THE LILY AND THE BULL

Books by Moyra Caldecott

FICTION
Guardians of the Tall Stones:
The Tall Stones
The Temple of the Sun
Shadow on the Stones
The Silver Vortex

Weapons of the Wolfhound
The Eye of Callanish
The Lily and the Bull
The Tower and the Emerald
Etheldreda
Child of the Dark Star
Hatshepsut: Daughter of Amun
Akhenaten: Son of the Sun
Tutankhamun and the Daughter of Ra
The Ghost of Akhenaten
The Winged Man
The Waters of Sul
The Green Lady and the King of Shadows

NON-FICTION/MYTHS AND LEGENDS
Crystal Legends
Three Celtic Tales
Women in Celtic Myth
Myths of the Sacred Tree
Mythical Journeys: Legendary Quests

CHILDREN'S STORIES
Adventures by Leaflight

THE LILY AND
THE BULL

a novel by
Moyra Caldecott

Published by
Bladud Books

First published in Great Britain in 1979 by Rex Collings Ltd.

This edition published in 2005 by
Bladud Books, an imprint of
Mushroom Publishing, Bath, UK

www.mushroompublishing.com

ISBN 1-84319-270-5

Printed and Bound by
Lightning Source

Contents

1

Encounter on the Mountain

Ierii had climbed much higher than she had intended, and clouds were lowering fast over the mountains, the peaks of solid rock disappearing into the whiteness, suggesting mysterious heights beyond their known limits.

She had been watching her sandalled feet on the rocks, continually sidestepping to avoid the sharp thorns of the bushes, when she suddenly noticed that the sun no longer warmed her skin and that she was cocooned in heavy mist. Her vision now could reach no further than her outstretched hand.

At first she was not worried, even though she had heard tales of people falling to their death in the mountains when the sky was hostile. She turned to descend, confident that she could find the way. She moved swiftly, sure that the quickly falling mist could not have hidden much of the path between herself and her home.

But she was wrong. The more she moved, the more completely she seemed to be enveloped.

She came to the sharp edge of a rock and found that it dropped away abruptly below her. A small stone that her foot dislodged slipped over the edge and was a long time falling.

She paused. For the first time the cold of the mist seemed to be inside her.

She did not remember this rock, this cliff. She shivered, feeling very much alone.

Surely she could not be far from familiar ground?

She tried to walk to the left, but the rocks were impassable. To the right she found a narrow passage, and carefully picked her way, trying fearfully every moment for safer footing.

By the time she found it she was a long way from where she thought she should have been. She remembered advice others had given: take no step upon the mountain if you cannot see. But if she did not move she might be there into the night.

It had become very cold, and her thin clothes were already damp. She cursed herself for being such a fool, setting off so impulsively without checking signs. The mountain always gave signs. The wind spoke. The birds could tell what weather was coming long before it came.

She had wanted to be alone, but not like this.

There were times when she could not stay in the town: times when she felt as though the thin veil that kept her separate as Ierii from the rest of the world no longer protected her, and all the loves, the hates, the pain, the anxieties of others were crowding in on her. At such times she would flee to the mountains, and in the quiet among the ancient rocks she would find herself again. But now she thought with nostalgia of the busy town on the plain far below her, between the mountains and the sea, and of Thyloss, whom she loved, but who she felt did not yet love her.

She stood still, the cold filaments of cloud touching her skin. But even as she neared despair, in the swirling whiteness that flowed everywhere about her, she felt the sudden haunting warmth of another's presence.

She could see no one.

She called. 'Who is there?'

She listened, but there was no answer. Perhaps the mist had muffled the sound of her voice. Her throat ached with tears she fought to keep from rising.

Then something moved above her, to the right. Anxiously, she strained to see through the mist.

Suddenly it seemed to part and, as clearly as if it were a

sunny day, she saw a woman of great beauty standing on a rock, shining from the mist like a white lily from the shade of leaves. She was taller than most women, her hair white as the moon, and her eyes dark and unfathomable. Ierii gasped, her hands at her mouth.

'It is the Lady herself!' she whispered. 'the Mother of the Earth!'

She was filled with awe, her heart beating so loudly and rapidly that she could feel it in her throat.

The woman beckoned, and Ierii moved without hesitation towards her. She found that she no longer stumbled over the stones, nor did the rough little thorn bushes tear at her legs.

She reached out to the woman she had never seen before, trustingly, as child to mother, but the mountain cloud swirled closer and the figure disappeared.

Ierii paused a moment, but the fear she had known before did not return. She moved forward with confidence, finding the ground beneath her feet level and secure.

When she reached the rock on which she had seen the woman standing, she found no one there, but when she looked down to the ground to see if there were any footprints to show that she had not imagined the presence of the Lady, she found the path that she had been seeking.

She wept freely, with relief and joy, and hurried down the mountain, her mind racing with the strange story that she would have to tell Thyloss and her father.

Would they believe that she had seen the Mother of the Earth, she, Ierii, fifteen summers old, not yet fledged to leave the nest and fly into the high realms of the Mysteries?

The town, Ma-ii, in which Ierii lived, and the palace it served, were built on a plain on the north coast of the island, a plain that now lay in bright sunlight although the mountains were in mist, the sea heaving quietly beside it, intensely blue.

At about the time Ierii started her descent from the mountain on the correct path, Thyloss, the son of Miron, was busy with other acrobats on the practice ground training on wooden blocks and bars for the complex leaps, somersaults and manoeuvres they would need when they faced the live bulls on the Field of Challenge. The young prince of Ma-ii, the only son of its formidable queen, was dead. The embalmers were busy in the palace; the acrobats preparing for the elaborate and dangerous funeral games.

Miron, Keeper of the Queen's Bulls, not knowing of the prince's death, had gone from town with several hunters on a routine search for wild bulls for the palace ceremonies, leaving his son Thyloss in charge of the bull enclosures and the men who tended them. It was to Thyloss therefore that the messenger came when there was trouble between two of the bulls.

Thyloss had not been pleased to be left to attend to his father's responsibilities and he uttered an exclamation of impatience when he was called in the middle of his practice. He was about to make an excuse for not going, when he noticed how breathless the youth who had brought the message was and how white-faced he looked. There was no avoiding it, he would have to go.

The narrow stone-flagged streets were quiet, and for the most part coolly shadowed by the houses. It was only when they came to open spaces at crossroads or in the market square that the white blaze of the sun hit the walls and ricocheted into their eyes. Thyloss was hot from his exertions on the training field and felt the sea breeze as it whistled down some of the streets cold and prickly on his skin.

'Hurry,' the youth cried anxiously, as Thyloss stopped for a moment at the corner of the Street of the Red Octopus and the Street of the Dolphin, to greet Ierii's father carrying an earthenware pot filled with shining red flowers and trailing vine-like leaves.

'Have you seen Ierii?' the man asked after the formal words of greeting, and Thyloss thought he detected a slight worried look in his eyes. He was surprised, for Dorran was noted for the calm, unhurried peacefulness of his nature, the gentle way he took all that life had to fling at him. In times past he had suffered much, but lately he and his daughter had lived together in great contentment, each day following the next, apparently in untroubled serenity.

'No, I have not. Should I?'

'1 feel uneasy,' Dorran said. 'She went to the mountains and the mist is down. I thought she might have returned early and been with you. She has more sense than to stay in the mountains when the mist . . .'

The messenger tugged Thyloss's sleeve.

'My lord . . .' he whispered anxiously.

'You will probably find her at home mixing her pigments for her wall paintings or wandering on the beach talking to the sea . . .' Thyloss said cheerfully to Dorran. There were a hundred places Ierii could be. She was one of those rare, quiet, private people who wandered abroad in the world freely and yet never seemed to touch it at all . . . almost as though, wherever she was, she was only partly there, the rest, the essential part, was in an unreachable world of her own. 'I must go,' the young man said in answer to another tug from the messenger and was already walking away as he called back over his shoulder: 'She will be all right. Do not worry.'

After this Thyloss and the messenger ran all the way to the bull enclosures, stopping for no one, though there were many who would have liked to pass the time of day with the handsome young athlete.

They found the area around the black bull's enclosure in an uproar. The air was thick with dust and the sound of hooves thudding and thundering, animals snorting and roaring. This combined with the shouting of the men to make a noisy, wild and confusing scene.

As soon as he appeared an old man rushed forward to meet him. It was Ayan, who, though officially retired as bull trainer and no longer permitted to handle the bulls or teach the acrobats, could not be persuaded to abandon the life he had enjoyed so much. Thyloss could see at once that he was the one most likely to give him a sensible explanation.

'What is it, Ayan?' he asked.

'The Black Thunderer and Grey Wind are at battle, my lord,' the old man said. 'Some fool boy left the gate open. Grey Wind got into the enclosure with the Black Thunderer and . . .'

Thyloss waited to hear no more.

He leapt up onto the wall and looked down into the dusty pen where the two giant bulls were lunging at each other. The most valuable bull of all, the Black Thunderer, the one chosen by Queen Nya-an for the funeral of her son, was covered with blood and dust and frothing sweat.

The earth shook as the two beasts pulled apart, turned, and charged at each other again and again. Thyloss felt himself choking on the red dust. Dimly he was aware of a group of children sitting in a row on the wall gleefully yelling encouragement to one bull or the other. They were not worried. It was a grand spectacle for them, and they cared nothing for the adult world of ritual and ceremony.

Several terrified youths were darting about the enclosure with long pronged rods trying to prize the two apart, or at least to distract them. The high-pitched warbling whistles that were customarily used to guide the bulls added to the noisy turbulence but had no effect on the enraged contestants.

Thyloss could see that Grey Wind's eyes were red as he turned for another attack. He was not as fine a bull as the Black Thunderer, his coat was not so silky nor his horns so white, but his powerful build was reminiscent of the rocky strength of the southern mountains from whence he came, and he was not going to give in.

The earth shook as the two charged and locked in battle yet again.

No wonder the Bull was believed to represent the destructive power of the earthquake, as well as the procreative power of Life. When Seers on the Island foresaw the danger of an earthquake, a bull, no matter how valuable, was sacrificed with elaborate ritual, the deathblow delivered with the deadly double axe, to placate the restless forces of the earth. It was only at funerals that the acrobats could show their skills and dance with the beast to show man's defiance of death, and his desire for new life.

As Thyloss stood on the wall of the enclosure, the small children turned their attention from the fighting bulls to him. He raised his voice in a high, long, and penetrating call, and his throat and mouth shaped a sound that belonged to the wild places of the earth.

He called again and again, the animal sound of his voice rising with each call and the final note so strange, so high and so rasping, that the other humans covered their ears and shuddered. The bulls paused in mid-charge and turned towards him with wide and staring eyes.

'Aa-aa-yi-yii-ee!' he wailed again, and leapt high and graceful as a swallow into the dusty pen, his feet scarcely touching ground before he was up again and flying with a leaping somersault over the back of the Black Thunderer.

Confused, the beast turned, but could not find the fleetly moving figure. He snorted and tossed his head.

Grey Wind stood still, breathing heavily, froth dripping from his jaw. Suddenly he turned and lumbered off, trying to find his way out. In the confusion he missed the gate and stumbled into the wall where the children were sitting. As he felt the stone wall smashing into his nose, he roared and snorted, his muscles rippling in preparation for the attack of this new enemy. The children, feeling his hot breath on their legs, and seeing his red eyes so close, squealed and fell backwards off the wall, a wriggling mass of arms and legs in the muck of the neighbouring empty bull pen.

Thyloss continued his dangerous dance while Grey Wind was distracted by some of the men. Swiftly and gracefully he leapt from side to side, turning the black bull one way and then the other. The animal lunged at his tormentor through the swirling dust, only to find the youth already behind him, mocking him with strange sounds.

The bull workers were no longer in panic. Thyloss knew

what he was doing and they respected him. They watched his every move while they held the large nets, waiting for the signal to throw them. They knew that when the time came they must make no mistakes.

'Now!' shouted Thyloss.

'Now!' echoed old Ayan, his rheumy eyes shining with excitement.

The bull workers rushed forward and flung the swirling nets over the two distraught beasts.

Tired and confused, the two animals did not know which way to turn, the nets entangling them as they were prodded and pushed from every side. At last the pain of their wounds began to tell and their resistance became less and less.

Grey Wind was led away, and the Black Thunderer was released at last to be left the sole occupant of his enclosure.

Then there were words of recrimination among the bull workers, each blaming the other for the incident. Above this noise rose the laughing voices of the children, who were extricating themselves from the muck and excitedly exchanging their impressions of the adventure.

Old Ayan and Thyloss brought back some kind of order.

Special herbs were called for and were boiled in great cauldrons. The liquid was then cooled slightly and poured over the wounds of the black bull. He did not like the sensation at first, but after a while he must have found it soothing, because he stood still, his eyes half closed.

'It will clean the wounds and help the healing,' Ayan said.

'Will he be ready for the prince's funeral?' Thyloss asked anxiously. He was wondering what the Queen would say if the Black Thunderer was not fit for the Challenge. It was the custom throughout the country for funerals, specially of important people, to be the occasion for a display of acrobatic skill against the bulls, the climax being the final challenge of one particular acrobat chosen by the family of the deceased to represent Life, and one particular bull chosen to represent Death, the two performing a deadly dance for the soul of the one whose champion the acrobat had become. It was only if the bull killed the acrobat that the mourning began in earnest. If the acrobat performed the challenge and survived, the funeral became a rejoicing. Life had won. The dead person would be soon reborn on this earth.

'The bull is healthy,' Ayan said. 'the herbs are strong. I see no reason why he should not be ready.'

'He will still be marked,' Thyloss said.

'Yes, he will still be marked,' Ayan agreed.

They were both silent.

He had been such a perfect bull, the most beautiful they had had in Ma-ii for a long time. Now one of his eyes was cut and the flesh around it was swelling rapidly. If his wounds did not heal well and exceptionally quickly, neither would like to take the responsibility of presenting him to the Queen.

Thyloss thanked Ayan for his help and gave stern orders to the rest of the bull workers, but blamed no one.

Wearily, as afternoon turned to evening, he walked back to his home. He would not be sorry when his father returned from the hunt.

On the path that led down from the mountains he met a be-draggled Ierii, her skirt torn and dirty, but her face shining with excitement.

'Thyloss, I must speak with you!' she cried.

'O no!' he groaned inwardly. He was exhausted. He was fond of Ierii and had been her closest friend for as long as either of them could remember, but he did not want to speak with anyone now. He had forgotten her father's earlier concern for her, he had forgotten the mist on the mountains, the possibility that she might have been in danger there. He could think of nothing but a pitcher of water over his head and a long cool drink.

Her dark eyes were looking into his eagerly and intensely. She was going to try to explain one of her strange thoughts to him. He was sure of it. He sighed. Usually he found Ierii's 'strange thoughts' fascinating, and many a time walking quietly along the beach with her, the water of the great ocean washing over their feet and the sky luminous with stars above them, he had felt that he was in the presence of someone very ancient and very wise, instead of a girl younger than himself with thin legs and a haunted, pale face. It was true the thin legs and the pale face were not much in evidence these days and lately he had found his attention distracted from what she had been saying by the full curve of her breast and the shine on her thick dark hair that reminded him of the blue-black sheen on the wing of a bird. But even her beauty, which still shone through now in spite of the dust and the disarray, could not distract him from his determination to cool down and rest.

'Ierii, not now,' he said wearily. 'I have no time now.' He had scarcely paused to listen to her, and plodded on past her as though she were some casual acquaintance whose expectation could be no more than a nod or a wave.

She stood still, gazing after him, the light fading from her eyes. She was hurt and shocked as though, bringing a gift, she had had it flung back in her face.

She bit her lip as she watched him moving gradually further and further from her. She could see that he had probably been working hard on the practice field for he was wearing only the short leather kilt that the acrobats wore for their work. His bronzed back was straight and strong, but his steps were dragging.

'He is very tired,' she told herself, trying not to dwell on the hurt, trying to find an excuse for his coldness towards her. But he had been tired before and yet he had always found time for her.

She turned for home, the joy of her recent experience marred by sadness.

Ierii's father, Dorran, like Thyloss's father Miron, was also a man of considerable importance in the community. He was Chief Gardener for the palace and lived in a beautiful house near its great southern entrance. From the wide northern windows of the upper storey of his home he could see the palace splendidly rising level upon level, the vines and creepers for which he was responsible spilling gracefully from window and balcony.

Gardens were not common in Ma-ii. The countryside was close enough for everyone to enjoy. The houses were built near each other: the streets were narrow and laid out so that the winds that blew so incessantly over the Island would not have free passage, and the shade of the buildings would give respite from the blazing summer sun.

The gardens people had were mostly indoors, in courtyards, on balconies, where they could keep them watered easily and out of reach of the fierce sun.

The palace of Ma-ii was famous for its courtyard and balcony gardens. Ierii's father was justly proud of his work. Ierii had grown up in a house that sometimes seemed like a forest, it was so full of cool green, for her father often grew the plants for the palace in his own home and only moved them to the great building when they were at their prime. Many of the noble families of the district consulted him, and many were the plants he had reared lovingly from seed that he later recognized in houses grander than his own.

The colonnaded paved court where Ierii and her father sat on summer evenings after the day's work was done was vivid with flowers. Creepers with rich and exotic blooms curled around the wooden columns. In every available space earthenware tubs and stone troughs stood, filled with a richly various foliage.

Dorran had even transplanted certain herbs that grew so freely in the mountains to their own little space beside the kitchen, so that Ierii would always have them available for cooking or healing.

Since Ierii was ten she had looked after her father. Her parents had been childless for many years and she had been born when they were already old and had given up hope of ever having a child. Her mother had prayed to the Goddess for a daughter, and had been told by the Seer who prophesied, that her prayer would be granted, but that she would enjoy the child for no more than ten years before they would be parted.

'Ten years with the daughter I love will be more to me than all the time the world has known,' Dorran's wife had said.

She bore a child, a daughter she called Ierii, which means 'answer to a prayer', but after the birth she never knew good health again.

On her mother's death, Ierii was left the responsibility of her father and her father's house.

Ierii's room looked to the mountains and her windows were framed with flowers, her wall rich with painted lilies.

Once one of her father's visitors had brought papyrus from Egypt for her, and she spent many happy days learning to draw the flowers that grew round her, transferring her designs painstakingly from the small pieces of papyrus to the large empty surfaces of the walls in the house. Her father encouraged her and often asked her to paint an unusual flower for him that he knew he would soon have to relinquish to the Queen.

Unlike most of the other houses in the town, theirs had a small piece of land behind it. There was a well, and at the edge of the garden on the south side there was a small, wild, rocky knoll where Ierii spent a great deal of her time, contemplating the beauty around her and thinking deeply about all that she saw.

Sometimes she felt that she was the most fortunate person in the world to have this private place, this small and secret mountain.

The official religion for some time had placed more and more emphasis on the Cult of the Bull, a representation of the powerful destructive force in nature worshipped in caves and underground chambers, and less and less on the Goddess, the subtle creative force that drove the tender shoot from seed to mighty tree, her representative, the Lady of the Lilies, worshipped in sacred groves and on the tops of mountains.

Somehow the understanding of Wholeness and Oneness had been lost, and the religious rituals which should have increased the feeling that the two great energies of the universe, the destructive and the creative, were dependent on each other, failed to do so. The followers of the Cult of the Bull feared and constantly placated a god they believed to be a Destroyer, while the Cult of the Lady cherished life in all its forms and on all its levels, but failed to satisfy the people who could see, but not understand, the harsh and violent side of the universe, the cleansing, winnowing action of nature.

When Ierii was a young child it was still possible for people to honour both the Goddess and the God, though even then they were thought of as separate beings representing separate and irreconcilable forces. She had once seen Queen Nya-an, chief priestess of the Bull Cult, carried up the Holy Mountain of the Lady, to visit the sanctuary of the Goddess. The child had been impressed to see the Queen step down from the portable throne of wood and ivory, to stand like any ordinary suppliant with hand to forehead before the invisible Presence, pleading for the life of her son. But though the boy had lived on he was constantly in such sickly health that the Queen's heart had hardened against the Divine Lady and the worship of the Goddess on the mountaintops was discouraged, all public religious rites confined to the palace and the Bull shrines.

The Bull games, as an important part of man's challenge of Death, and the Bull sacrifice offered in times of danger to the Earth Shaker, the Great Destroyer, were so much part of the Island's tradition that no one questioned them. If anyone noticed that the gentler, more receptive and intuitive side of their religion was gradually disappearing, no one proclaimed it from the rooftops. The Queen was hard and fierce, her hand was over Ma-ii like a dark cloud. Her very name, Nya-an, was a name of ominous power. Nya-an, Shadow of the Bull.

From an early age Ierii had watched the Bull games with

excitement. The skill and daring of the acrobats were magnificent, and, of course, being in love with Thyloss, they had an added interest for her.

But she had no sense of a Divine Presence at any of the rituals of the Bull Cult. She had no feeling that the ceremonial games were anything more serious than a challenge of skills between animal and man. She hated the Bull sacrifices, and usually managed to avoid attending them. But she had not admitted even to her father the blasphemous thoughts she had about their lack of purpose. It seemed everyone else accepted them as an important part of their religion. Were there not shrines with horns all about her?

Strangely, her own house did not have one. She thought of this, and wondered about it as she turned for home now, anxious to tell her father about her experience on the mountain.

He would listen, she thought, even if Thyloss had not. She found him digging a trench for some new and unusual plants the latest ship from the East had brought to Ma-ii. He was very excited about them and anxious to get them planted.

'Look!' he cried as soon as he saw her, and he held up the roots for her to admire. They were huge, and Ierii wondered what kind of monstrous flower would grow from them.

'I have promised one to my old friend Ayan,' her father said. 'And I shall keep one, but the others, of course, must go to the palace.'

'The Queen might not like them,' Ierii said, only half concentrating, eager to turn the conversation to her own experience.

'She will like them!' cried her father. 'She will be pleased to have something no other palace in the country has.'

'Father,' said Ierii thoughtfully.

'Pass me that jug of water,' the old man said, not noticing that she had something to tell him.

'Father,' repeated Ierii loudly and more purposefully, holding the jug for him. 'What would you think if I were to tell you that I had seen the Goddess and that she had saved my life?'

'Not so much,' remonstrated her father, as she absentmindedly tipped the jug. 'We do not want to drown them. They come from a very dry country, you know.'

'Father, you are not listening to me!' Ierii's voice sounded so insistent, even the excited old man had to stop what he was doing to look at her in surprise.

'The Goddess . . . the Mother of the Earth! I saw her!'

'Where?' His voice was cautious.

'On the mountain. I was lost in the mist and she appeared to me and showed me the way down. I might have died.'

'I told you not to go into the mountains without seeing which way the wind is bending that tree.' the old man straightened his back and pointed to a small tree on Ierii's rocky knoll.

'But, Father – that is not the point! Do you not understand what I am saying?'

He listened to her story then, and thought about what she had said.

He sat on the step and forgot about his new plants. His eyes were withdrawn. He was remembering the time his wife, who, they thought, was past the age of childbearing, had asked for a child, and had been given one.

The Goddess had already showed interest in Ierii, it was not impossible that she should show it again.

They sat together on the warm stone step for some time, thinking and gazing at the cloud-covered mountains.

Ierii had seen what no one she had ever known had seen.

The Queen might do what she liked about the Cult of the Bull, but she, Ierii, would hold to the old religion, the faith older than time itself, the Spirit that gave birth to the earth, and walked their mountains now clad in the body of a woman, watching over them as mother watches over child. She felt at peace with the Goddess. Afraid of the fierce Lord of the Bulls.

'Is it not a wonderful thing that I have seen her, Father?' Ierii asked dreamily, happily.

'I wonder,' the old man said musingly.

'I have seen her, Father!'

'Mist plays strange tricks,' he said gently.

'Father, I saw her!'

'You saw a woman, my child. How can you be sure that she was the Goddess?'

'She was so . . . beautiful . . . so old . . . and so young at the same time . . . and the way she appeared and . . . disappeared.'

'It is possible that it was not the Goddess at all, but . . .' the old man seemed to be pursuing another line of thought, though he did not continue it aloud.

'Who, then?' demanded Ierii.

He shook his head, and his expression showed that he did not want to continue the conversation.

There was something he did not want to tell Ierii.

He returned to his mud and his roots and would talk no more. Ierii went to her room, washed herself with the sweet well water from the jug that always stood there, and lay down on her bed.

I will go again, she thought fiercely to herself. I will find her. I will bring back a sign that no one will be able to doubt.

The painted lilies on the walls of her room seemed to glow as the last light of the dying sun touched them.

2

The Queen 'Honours' Thyloss

The following morning the Queen summoned Thyloss to the palace.

She was not in the megaron, where she usually gave audience, but was in one of her private apartments.

As he climbed the stairs to the upper floor and followed one of her women attendants through the narrow and labyrinthine passages to her rooms, he was nervous. Had she heard about the fight of the bulls? In a close community such as theirs it would not have taken long for reports of such an unusual event to reach her ears.

She was in her day room, the screens that kept the weather out in winter were drawn back and almost the whole side of the room was open to the free-flowing air and a view of the distant sea. The plants that grew so profusely in pots between the columns stirred gently in a cooling breeze.

She was not alone. Her four closest attendants were sitting at her feet. The scent they wore and the scent of the flowers was strong, and Thyloss found himself swallowing rapidly several times, overwhelmed by female beauty and female presence.

He bowed his head to her with conventional respect, but then held it high. He had never been one to humble himself before anyone. If he was blamed for the injuries to the Black Thunderer, he would accept the responsibility boldly.

The Queen stared at him long and hard. Her eyes, lined and shaped with kohl, were like black glass.

Her women rose and moved around him, gazing at him

as though he were on show, whispering among themselves as some particular thing about him caught their attention.

The Queen watched, her eyes narrowed, a faint smile on her lips. His resentment amused her. His tall and handsome body aroused her.

But most of all, his pride and inner strength pleased her. She was tired of men who were afraid of her. Her own husband never spoke to her without lowering his eyes.

'You are Thyloss, the son of my lord, the Keeper of the Bulls,' she said at last.

'My lady, you know that I am,' he answered, meeting her eyes.

The women around him withdrew slightly, tittering. A flicker of irritation crossed the Queen's face. She raised her arm and made a gesture of dismissal to them. They left at once, their long skirts swirling as they passed through the door into the adjoining room.

Thyloss felt more at ease when they were gone. They had the bodies of women, full-breasted and seductive, but the minds and behaviour of children.

The woman before him was no fool. She had a formidable mind and an unshakeable will. Her power in the land was considerable.

He met her stare as he would that of a bull he was about to challenge. Her gaze never wavered. He would not break the silence, though he longed for release from her scrutiny. At last she moved, and gestured for him to be seated.

But he remained standing.

The stool was at her feet.

Amused, she nodded.

'You take a risk, sir. Have you forgotten who I am?'

'No, my lady. But what you have to say would be better said quickly. We both know that.'

'And what is it that I have to say?' she asked mockingly. Thyloss flushed. Why did she play with him?

At last he could bear no more and bowed his head slightly, acknowledging her rebuke and indicating that he was ready to listen. She smiled and rose from her chair.

His eyes followed her as she paced about the room, and he began to wonder if he had been correct in thinking that she had called him to berate him about the Black Thunderer. There was something about her that suggested to him that she was finding it difficult to say what she wanted to say.

He waited.

At last she came to rest in front of him.

She was his height and her eyes looked directly into his.

'Thyloss,' she said, using his given name as though she had known him all his life. 'Thyloss, I have decided to do you a great honour. Three great honours,' she corrected herself.

He said nothing, but he could feel his heart pounding now.

'Do you not want to know what they are?' she asked impatiently.

'Yes, my lady,' he said with a dry throat.

She smiled and looked more relaxed.

'The first honour I give you is to be the one to challenge the Black Thunderer at the funeral of my son.'

With the relief beads of sweat broke out on Thyloss' forehead.

He bowed.

It was indeed an honour.

He had recently won great acclaim as an acrobat, but he had not realized that he had been accepted as one of the foremost, to be entrusted with the role of Life's champion at a royal funeral.

A second thought struck him. Did this mean she had not heard what had happened to the Black Thunderer? But he decided not to refer to it unless she did.

'I am grateful,' he said in a low voice.

'So you should be,' she said brusquely, and then, when the silence became uncomfortable between them once more, she said: 'Do you not want to hear what else I have planned for you?' It seemed to him that her eyes sparkled strangely as she looked into his.

'Of course, my lady,' he muttered, uneasily.

'I have decided the usual funeral rituals are not enough for my son. After the Challenge' – and a slight edge of wariness had come to her voice as though she realized he would not be so eager to accept this second honour – 'you will be the one to plunge the double axe into the forehead of the Black Thunderer.'

'My lady!' He looked shocked and startled. Not only was it unusual to sacrifice a bull at a funeral, but when a sacrifice was called for it had always been the prerogative of the priestesses of the Bull Cult to perform the ceremony.

'What do you think of that?' she said, her eyes sparkling at his discomfiture. She was amused by the conflicting emotions she could read in his face. 'As my son's champion,' she continued, 'you will challenge the Black Thunderer and win. Death will be defied. The prince's rebirth will be assured. And then I will give him a gift. I will give him the greatest bull this palace has ever known to take with him on his journey from one life to another. He will ride in triumph through the regions of the Shades and will be worshipped as a god when he returns to earth. He will challenge the Lady of the Lilies once and for all. He will shake the earth with his rage. His strength will be as great as the force that began the world!'

Thyloss looked at her in astonishment.

Was she mad?

Her son? the feeble prince! Who, when he was alive, had been a stupid, snivelling boy who was so dull-witted that he even found it necessary to cheat at games played with counters!

The Queen's face glowed with pride as she thought of her son.

Thyloss lowered his eyes, lest she should see his thoughts in them.

'And . . .' she continued, noticing that her words had had an effect upon him, though she did not read it correctly, 'after the funeral, and the presentation of the gift of the bull to my son's soul, there will be a royal wedding.'

Thyloss looked up, startled.

'Yes, my dear, that is the third honour I do you! You are to marry my daughter Meri-an, heir to my throne.'

She looked at him triumphantly, her eyes blazing with excitement at her vision of the future.

Thyloss was dumbfounded.

Memories came to him of the princess, delicate and pale, and still no more than twelve summers old, sitting beside her mother at palace ceremonies. Whenever he had heard speculations about her marriage it had always been in connection with the princes of royal blood who visited Ma-ii from other palaces. He was amazed that he should be considered for such an honour. His thoughts changed direction with every moment that passed in silence between the queen and himself. He was at once flattered and tempted, and yet at the same time appalled. The constrictions of life as the consort of a queen would not suit him, and the thought that he would be continually beside that pale, quiet child and no longer with Ierii and his lively friends of the Bull games was a disturbing one.

'My lady, why do you choose me?' he asked cautiously.

She smiled, pleased with what she thought was his humility.

'Because I have chosen you,' she said with satisfaction, as though there could be no other explanation necessary.

'But why?' he persisted.

Her face clouded.

'Do I, the queen, have to give reasons?' she thundered.

He was silent.

'Well?' she said at last, when he still did not speak. 'What have you to say?'

He took a deep breath.

Dare he say, 'No, I will not do it'?

Dare he?

Her cold eyes were watching him . . . snake goddess . . . all destructive powers poised to strike.

Where was the Dove, the woman-mother?

'I cannot,' he said in a low voice, too low for her to hear.

'What?' Her word cracked like a whip over him.

'I cannot,' he said more loudly, lifting his head, gathering strength.

'Cannot!' she almost screamed.

He was startled at the change in her, the lack of control. Why was it so important to her that he should dance with the Black Thunderer, take the place of a priestess to sacrifice the animal against tradition and custom, and marry the young princess who would one day be queen?

Why?

'You will do it!' she said, her voice the most deadly he had ever heard, her eyes cutting into him in a way that he would not have thought possible.

She was queen.

Not woman.

Snake queen.

Bull queen.

High Priestess of the Dark Lord, the Destroyer. Wielder of the earthquake and the storm!

'I will do it,' he heard his voice saying, though his heart was crying for what he would lose.

He found himself trembling. He, Thyloss, the most fearless challenger of bulls, now stood defeated.

'Go!' she commanded, pointing to the door.

He went.

3

Second Encounter on the Mountain

While Thyloss was at the palace Ierii made her way back to the mountain. This time she consulted all the signs, and impatient as she was, she really believed that she would not have gone had the omens been against it.

But luckily all was well. The tree her father had told her to use as wind guide scarcely stirred. The birds were flying high and singing freely.

She intended to spend the whole day, for she realized that it might not be easy to find the mysterious and beautiful Lady she had glimpsed so fleetingly. She carried a pouch with bread and fruit. The grapes and oranges would provide liquid if she found no water.

All morning she climbed and at noon she was on a high ridge. She could see the town of Ma-ii lying snugly on the sea plain far below her, the waters of the ocean, deep blue and flecked with white. How lovely the scene was; like a setting for the palace that gleamed jewel-like at its centre. How slow and timeless the pace of life seemed from this distance.

'Forever' seemed an easy concept to grasp.

'Forever' the sea carrying their ships to distant lands.

'Forever' the palace ruling in peaceful wisdom.

'Forever' artists painting, weavers weaving, potters making pots, cooks cooking, smiths fashioning bronze.

Ierii sat awhile and ate some bread and grapes. They were good. The grapes were from the vine that grew on the south wall of their house, and had ripened early with the best of the sun and the least of the wind.

She felt a shadow flick over her and looked up, surprised. She had seen no clouds.

A pair of golden eagles was circling high above her, their wings briefly obscuring the sun as their arc took them between her and the golden disc.

She strained her eyes to see them better, the one lower than the other.

Had they seen her? She felt that they were watching her, and a chill came to her heart.

Mountains, she knew, were places you did not lightly face alone. On the bare rock of the mountain summit you could not hide behind your fellow men, the walls of your home, the regalia of your office. You were exposed, whoever you were, small and frail, to the mystery of all mysteries, the question that seemed to have no answer.

Was it for this reason people had always found it a natural place to worship?

'Mother of the Earth . . . Lady of the Lilies . . . come to me,' she whispered, watching the eagles turn and turn again, their wings scarcely moving as the currents of air carried them in two slow spirals.

But if she had been the object of their attention, she was no longer. She noticed the spiral did not centre on her and their lowering gaze was fastened on something in the valley beyond her. She shivered slightly with relief and picked up her belongings.

The ridge was high, but it was not where she expected to find the Lady. It dipped slightly to the east and then rose to form a cluster of jagged peaks, pitted with caves and bare of trees. It was there that she estimated she had seen the figure in the mist, and it was there that she would seek the Goddess now.

The sun was hot, but as she climbed a strong wind came suddenly whipping from between the peaks and she found herself having to lean into it to keep her balance. Her skirts flapped, her long black hair was torn from the gold pins that normally secured it, and beat the air like the wings of a trapped bird. Sometimes the long strands stung her eyes and temporarily blinded her.

But she did not give up.

She could not find the exact place where she had seen the Lady of the Mountain and almost began to believe that she had imagined the experience. Tears came to her eyes as she looked at the sun and knew that it was well into its descent and that she must turn back if she did not want to face a night alone on the mountain.

She had no proof to take to her doubting father and to ungracious Thyloss, but from time to time on her quest she had had the very strong impression that she was not alone, that she was being watched.

Even as she turned to go home, she fancied she heard a movement and felt a Presence.

She turned towards it, but she saw no one.

'Lady!' she called, making one last effort.

The echo came back to her, soft as a sigh. She waited. Nothing. No one.

Sadly she picked her way over rock and scrubby bush, back down to the plain and the town, to the noise and the bustle of people.

Quiet as a shadow, a figure stood watching her, the late-afternoon sunlight falling on hair that shone like silver.

When Ierii reached home, tired and discouraged, she was upset to hear that Thyloss had been to the house looking for her.

'Oh no!' she cried, disappointed, for it had been some time since Thyloss had sought her out.

They had been close friends for almost as long as she could remember and had always shared each other's sorrows and triumphs. But lately a change had come in her feelings towards him. She longed for him as lover, not as friend. Sadly, his feelings for her did not seem to have suffered the same change.

'What did he say?' she asked her father eagerly, forgetting her weariness.

'Nothing. As soon as he heard that you were not here, he went away.' And then he seemed to recall something. 'He seemed agitated. He did not even say goodbye to me,' he added, slightly aggrieved. He had always liked Thyloss and had been disappointed when he had recently noticed his daughter's yearning for the young acrobat was not being fully reciprocated.

Ierii thought hard. She had not the patience to wait until the morning to speak with him, and she rushed to her room, washed, and put on fresh clothes. She took an outdoor lamp and hurried off down the rapidly darkening streets.

'Ierii!' called her father. 'You have not eaten!'

But she did not hear him.

The house of the Keeper of the Queen's Bulls was at the eastern edge of the town, not far from the enclosures where the bulls were kept.

Ierii had to pass a great many households settling down for the evening meal. The delicious cooking smells nearly drove her wild. She was hungry. But she was also very anxious to see Thyloss. What could have happened since yesterday when he had treated her so coolly?

He was not at home when she arrived, but his sister thought that he was at the bull enclosures.

'He is worried about the Black Thunderer,' she explained.

Ierii looked hungrily past her shoulder at the table laid for dinner, the rest of the family sitting peacefully around it ready to eat.

'Eat with us,' the sister said kindly, seeing Ierii's look. 'Wait for him. He will probably not be long.'

Ierii hesitated. The food looked very good, but she wanted to see Thyloss.

Thyloss' mother rose from the table and brought some food to Ierii.

'Here, my dear, take it, eat . . . but go and find Thyloss. I am worried about him. He has been behaving very strangely today. But he will not tell any of us what the matter is. Perhaps he will tell you.'

She took the food gratefully and ate it as she hurried to the black bull's enclosure.

When she found Thyloss he was sitting on the wall staring gloomily into the dark.

'Thyloss,' she called to him, softly, half afraid she would not be welcome, but this time his face in the flickering flame of the lantern looked relieved to see her.

He leapt down, gracefully, and stood before her.

'Ierii,' he said, 'I need your help.'

She flushed with pleasure, glad of the dark so that he could not see her expression.

'What has happened?'

'What has not happened!' he said despairingly.

He seemed to have forgotten that he had been trying to discourage their friendship since he had sensed the change in her interest in him, and returned to treating her as the good friend she had always been.

He took her over to a fallen tree trunk and they sat down side by side. She shivered slightly with the evening cold, but was reluctant to snuggle up to him for warmth as she might have done when they were children.

'What is it?' she prompted, as he did not seem to know where to begin.

He hesitated a moment longer and then, as the sky darkened, the stars became brighter and more numerous, and their lamp flickered and went out, he told her what had happened at the palace that morning.

She was glad they were in the dark and so she could let her feelings play freely in her face without his taking offence. At first there was pride and joy at the honour of his being chosen to challenge the Black Thunderer, but mingled with it was the fear that he would be harmed, possibly even killed. The mention of the sacrifice of the bull at the end of the funeral bewildered her, but even this was driven from her mind when Thyloss mentioned his betrothal to the young princess. She had seen the princess. She was beautiful beyond words. 'But cold as ice!' Ierii added fiercely to herself. 'Cold! No life in her at all! Besides, she is just a child!' And she thought of her as she had seen her in processions in the palace ceremonies, a pale shadow behind her tall and magnificent mother. She was like a pearl, a jewel with no fire in its heart.

'Are you listening?' Thyloss suddenly said suspiciously. There had been no sound from her for a long time.

'I cannot believe it,' she said hastily, trying to control the first stirrings of jealousy before they became unmanageable.

'I keep telling myself it cannot be,' Thyloss said. 'But what am I to do if she really meant it? And why is she doing it? Why? Why me?'

'I should have thought why she has chosen you was obvious. You are much handsomer than any prince on the Island.'

'Nonsense. Besides, it is not common for the future queen to marry someone not of the royal line.'

'It has been known to happen.'

There was silence between them for a while, and when Thyloss spoke again at last, his voice was very troubled.

'Ierii, what am I to do?' he said.

'Do you want to marry the princess?'

'Of course not . . . I mean . . . I do not know . . . I do not know what she is like . . .'

Thyloss felt Ierii's eyes on him in spite of the darkness.

'Curse it all . . . I do not want to marry anyone!'

His voice was quite angry.

But even more than the marriage, the sacrifice of the bull worried him, and he spoke to Ierii about this now.

She thought about it deeply.

'It is very strange,' she said quietly.

She thought about the Goddess she had seen on the mountain . . . the beautiful, strong, compassionate face. She could not imagine her delighting in blood sacrifice.

Could the Queen do what she had planned? Could she, by sacrificing a bull to her puny dead son as though he were a god, change the ancient truths?

'You would not listen to me yesterday Thyloss,' she said softly but firmly. 'Listen now. It may be of great importance.'

She told him about the encounter on the mountain. He was silent, listening very carefully.

'What are you saying?' he said at last.

'I am saying the Goddess is real. I have seen her. Let us go and ask her what to do.'

'But today you could not find her?'

'She was there. I felt her Presence. I just could not see her.'

Thyloss thought about it. He really had great respect for Ierii. Even as a very young girl she had 'known' things in a way that other people did not know them, and he had learned to listen to her 'feelings'.

What had he to lose? No ordinary person could help him, except possibly his father, but he was far from home. The prince had still been alive when Miron left for the hunt and since he could not know of the royal death he would see no reason to hurry back.

In the morning Thyloss made sure the Black Thunderer was attended to: his wounds were healing rapidly. He left Ayan in charge, and set off to join Ierii.

But it was not to be. On the way to her house he was intercepted and summoned to the palace.

'I cannot come,' he said firmly to the messenger. 'Convey my regrets.'

'My lady was very insistent. She will not accept refusal.'

Thyloss hesitated.

'How did she look? Angry or happy?'

The messenger thought about it.

'Her face was very stiff. I cannot tell. Her daughter was with her and —' here he hesitated, wondering if he should betray so much '— and . . . she had been weeping.'

A spark of hope came to Thyloss. If the princess was against the marriage, perhaps her mother would change her mind. He decided it would be foolish not to fan this spark.

'I will come,' he said, 'but you must take a message to someone for me.'

'Willingly,' said the lad, relieved that he would not have to convey Thyloss' refusal back to the Queen.

'Go to the house of Dorran, the lord Gardener, and ask to speak with his daughter Ierii. She will be waiting for me and . . .' Thyloss looked at the boy with a slight flicker of sympathy. 'She will probably cry. Tell her as gently as you can that I cannot come, that I am sorry, but that I want her to find the lady she mentioned and ask the questions we arranged to ask. Can you remember all that? It is important.'

'Yes, of course,' the boy said.

'Remember' – Thyloss looked at him closely – 'it is important.'

'I will remember.'

'Go quickly, then . . . I have already kept her waiting long enough.'

The boy turned at once to go. Thyloss watched him, and then turned with a heavy heart to follow the path to the palace.

Ierii was indeed upset, but she did not cry.

The boy did not intend to tell her anything more than he had been instructed to, but Ierii managed to extract from him the fact that Thyloss had been summoned to the palace.

This made her indignant and at first she felt like abandoning her mission to the mountains and abandoning Thyloss to the princess. But . . . her feelings for Thyloss were too strong. She thanked the boy and dismissed him.

She knew her father was at the palace and would be very busy there until after the funeral – and the wedding! She added this thought with a touch of bitterness. He would not have time to wonder where she had gone. She took food, and this time a cloak, in case she could not return before nightfall.

Indeed she did not reach the rocky outcrops and the caves until well into the afternoon. She did not stop there, but continued purposefully towards the summit.

The mountain wind was cold and she was glad of her

cloak, but her pouch of food felt heavier and heavier as her limbs became weary. Her desire to reach the summit was now so obsessive that she felt no hunger, and before long she loosened the thong that held the pouch to her hip and abandoned it on a ledge.

When at last she reached as high as she could go, she stopped and lifted her arms and her eyes to the sky. She said nothing, but let the longing in her heart speak for itself.

The sky took her.

She could feel its immensity accepting her into itself.

She was no longer Ierii, and, as though in a dream, took off the wristlet with her seal stone and laid it reverently on the rock.

How strange that she had thought Ma-ii and all that happened there so important.

She looked down upon the plain that she had left that morning and found that it had changed.

The town was gone.

Earth covered her home and all that she had known. The sea still lapped the white sands of the shore, but goats cropped yellow daisies in quiet fields that were now where the great palace had once so proudly stood.

She tried to recall names, but they eluded her.

Only the wind's voice was in her ears, and the wind spoke no names.

She shuddered as the vision began to fade and she was aware of herself on the mountaintop again.

But she was not alone. Beside her was the Lady she had sought.

The woman looked at her with great compassion for a time and then stepped forward, stooped to retrieve the seal stone, and bound it gently upon the girl's wrist.

'You are flesh and blood!' Ierii whispered.

The woman smiled.

'Is that such a terrible thing to be?'

'No,' stammered Ierii, 'I meant . . . I thought . . .'

'We think many things,' the woman said gently.

'Who are you?' Ierii pleaded, after the silence between them had helped her to recover her composure slightly.

'Come, I will take you home,' the woman said, taking Ierii's hand and leading her down.

'I do not want to go home yet,' Ierii said. 'I need to talk with you.'

'My home,' the woman said simply.

Ierii was quiet then and followed eagerly. Gradually she gained confidence to give words to her curiosity.

'I thought you were the Mother of the Earth, the Goddess . . .' she ventured.

The woman walked on and did not reply.

'Are you?' Ierii could contain herself no longer.

The woman paused and turned to her.

'My name is Quilla,' she said simply.

The name teased Ierii's mind. She felt that she had heard it before, but could not remember where.

She tried to think as they walked on, but it would not come to her.

At last they stopped before a cave, the entrance to which was protected and half hidden behind a rough stone wall which had probably been built as a windbreak, for the cave entrance faced straight into the path of the prevailing wind. Ierii was astonished that she had missed it the day before.

Inside it was cool and pleasant, with curtains woven from black and white goat hair hung over the walls for extra comfort.

Ierii had not realized that she was as tired as she was until Quilla suggested she should relax on a pallet of soft straw.

'Rest,' Quilla said kindly. 'You have travelled farther than you know. Sleep if you can. I will prepare food.'

Ierii did not want to sleep. She had too many questions to ask, but Quilla touched her head and with her touch drowsiness came over the girl and she could not stay awake.

She woke with a start and found herself still in the cave.

Quilla was seated cross-legged before a low fire, gazing into its depths. Night had fallen. When Ierii moved, the woman turned to her and smiled encouragingly.

'Do not be afraid. You are safe.'

Ierii looked about her, the flames making strange dancing patterns on the uneven walls of rock. The worries about Thyloss and herself that she had so strangely lost when she stood on the mountaintop suddenly came back to her. She sat up.

Could she ask this woman for advice, even though she was not, as she had hoped, the Goddess?

'Eat first, and drink,' Quilla said as though she had read her thoughts. 'And then we will talk.'

The food was good. The broth of herbs and nettles warming and tasty. Ierii began to feel peaceful and refreshed. She found it easy to speak to the beautiful woman.

'How is it that I have heard your name and yet cannot recall what I have heard?' she asked at last.

'I was known in Ma-ii and in all the palaces of the Island once – but that was long ago – when your father and mother were still young.'

'Did you know my mother?' Ierii asked eagerly.

'I have met her, but I did not know her well. You look much like her.'

Ierii flushed with pleasure.

'Forgive me, Lady . . . but I still cannot recall what I have heard about your name.'

'You have a friend who is an acrobat I think?'

'Yes,' cried Ierii, surprised that she should know about Thyloss.

'Ask him if the name of Quilla means anything to him. Ask old Ayan, who still works with bulls although he should be living quietly now, an honoured guest of those who want to hear rich tales of earlier days.'

'Were you an acrobat?' Ierii asked.

Quilla smiled.

'Yes, I was an acrobat,' she said simply.

Ierii was silent. If she had been known in all the palaces

she must have been a very famous one. Only the very exceptional were called upon to perform before other thrones.

'Why do you live alone here, in a cave? You speak of Ayan, yet you should be living in the town, greatly cared for and admired.'

Quilla laughed aloud at this, and rose to put more wood on the fire.

'You think so?' she asked, with a touch of mockery in her voice. Ierii flushed. What was so wrong in that?

'Did you learn nothing on the mountaintop?' Quilla asked.

Ierii looked puzzled. Quilla could see that she was not yet ready to understand all that had been shown her in the vision. She sat down in front of her and spoke to her gently and patiently.

'What did you feel on the mountaintop?'

Ierii tried to recall.

'Why did you put down your seal stone?' Quilla prompted.

'Because . . . because . . . I felt that I was no longer Ierii . . . but somehow . . . I could see everything . . .'

'What did you see?'

'I saw Ma-ii.'

'Was it as you saw it when you left it this morning?'

'No . . . it was as though . . . as though it was buried deep in the earth.'

Ierii's eyes were bewildered as she again saw the vision she had seen.

'And where were you?'

'I . . . I do not know . . .'

'You must have been there to see what you saw?'

'I . . . I suppose so. I felt . . . I mean . . . I "saw" . . . but I could not see myself.'

'Did you feel sorrow because Ma-ii was no more?'

'No. I do not think so.'

'What did you feel?'

'I do not know how to express it. I saw it – but I thought nothing of it. It was just part of everything – neither good nor bad.'

'And you were there "thinking" that, "feeling" that, "seeing" that?'

'Yes.'

'So Ma-ii was no more. But you were?'

Ierii began to grasp what Quilla was trying to teach.

'Yes.'

'That is why you felt no sorrow. You saw Ma-ii and all its splendours as only temporary, but yourself as eternal.'

Ierii thought about how she had experienced consciousness and yet had had no personal identity or body with which to associate it.

'And what of this boy you love?' Quilla looked straight into Ierii's eyes.

'I did not see him.'

'Did you feel his presence with you?'

Ierii was trying to remember. It was very difficult.

'Did you think of him lying under the earth with the buildings of Ma-ii, or did you think of him still existing like you?'

'He was not in the town . . .' Ierii said hesitantly. 'I remember!' she suddenly cried joyfully. 'Because I had put my seal stone down I was no longer Ierii . . . I was no longer separate from Thyloss or anyone else who is living. I . . . "we" . . . were together looking at the place where the town had been. We felt no regret because what we had lost was only the shadow of what we had gained.'

'You see!' Quilla cried triumphantly. 'You have the answers to all your questions already!'

Ierii looked puzzled. It was true she had fleetingly grasped something very important, but now she was confused.

How did all this help her to sort out the immediate problem?

'Tell me, what is troubling you?' Quilla asked.

Ierii poured out the whole story. Her love for Thyloss, his problem with the Queen . . .

Quilla looked very grave while Ierii told her about the Queen's conversation with Thyloss, and was thoughtfully silent a long time after she had finished speaking.

'What should we do?' asked Ierii at last, unable to contain her anxiety any longer.

Quilla shook her head and Ierii knew that she must be quiet a while longer.

'You asked me why I live in a cave in the mountains?' Quilla said at last.

'Yes,' said Ierii.

'There are several reasons, but one of the most important is that I grew weary of living amongst the short-sighted and the blind. There are things I can see as clearly as I can see the flames in the fire . . . and yet no one will listen to me . . . no one cares . . .'

'I will listen! I care!' cried Ierii.

'I know that . . . that is why I showed myself to you . . . that is why I brought you here.'

Quilla seemed to be thinking again, and Ierii did not interrupt her, but waited patiently, pleased by what she had said.

At last Quilla spoke again, but more as though she were speaking to herself than to Ierii.

'The love of Miron and myself plays a role in these events . . .'

Here Ierii jumped with surprise. Miron, the Keeper of the Queen's Bulls, the father of Thyloss?

'Jealousy drove Nya-an to condemn me and banish me . . . and now she seeks my son for her daughter . . .'

Ierii's eyes were wide open.

Thyloss?

Was Thyloss Quilla's son?

But Thyloss had a mother, Miron's wife.

Ierii thought about Thyloss and his family. She had always been surprised how like his father he was but how different from the rest of his family, who were pleasant enough, but ordinary. Thyloss was like a god to them. Even his 'mother,' Miron's wife, treated him with the respect due an honoured stranger.

Quilla was still talking and Ierii tried hard to bring her mind back to concentrate on the Lady's words.

'She goes too far . . .' she was murmuring. 'She goes too far! She deprived me of the man I love. She cannot have my son! And to use him in such a way! To break with tradition and the laws of ritual . . . and to make him perform a blood sacrifice when no sacrifice is called for. It is wrong! No good will come of it.'

Quilla was in great distress and Ierii was sad to have been the cause of it.

'Perhaps it is the time . . .' Quilla's brow furrowed with anxiety. 'the time I have been warned about . . . the end of Ma-ii . . .'

Ierii looked startled and alarmed.

'My lady?' She could hold still no longer.

Quilla seemed suddenly to remember Ierii's presence and to recover her former calm.

'You must not fear it,' she said gently, looking deep into the girl's eyes. 'You have seen that Ma-ii is nothing. Your life is not tied to it.'

'But it is my home,' Ierii cried, and her heart ached suddenly for her little room of flowers, her garden, the rocky knoll where she had spent so much time . . .

The lady Quilla bent toward Ierii and kissed her softly on the forehead.

'Your only true home is in there,' she said, touching with her finger the place she had kissed. 'And when you are released from your body, it expands until you are within it.'

She could see Ierii did not understand.

'No matter,' she said with a smile. 'there will be time enough for you to grasp these things.'

Ierii looked at her for a moment in silence.

There was something else that worried her in the woman's words – perhaps that would be easier to grasp.

'My lady,' she said diffidently. 'Do I understand that Thyloss is your son?'

'Did I say that?' Quilla asked.

'Yes, you did.'

'I spoke the truth. He is my son!' Quilla declared.

Ierii caught her breath.

Her head rang with questions, but she could see from Quilla's expression that it would not be right to ask them.

'Thyloss is also the son of Miron. And Miron was once much loved by the Queen. That is why she has chosen Thyloss for her daughter. He is Miron's son and so, with her own son dead, she has chosen the only one who could come near to taking his place.'

'Must he marry the princess, Meri-an?' Ierii asked sadly. 'Is there no way to prevent it?'

'Much will happen in the next few days, child of a prayer, and nothing that is planned by the Queen will necessarily happen exactly as she wishes.'

'Does that mean . . .?' Ierii's face lit up.

'You ask too many questions, and I do not know all the answers. Be at rest now. I am tired.'

Quilla indeed looked tired, and older than she had seemed before.

'Sleep now – and in the morning return to Ma-ii . . . warn everyone to leave the town and to seek sanctuary in the mountains and beyond . . . the days of Ma-ii are over.'

She raised her hand and touched Ierii's forehead.

The bewildered girl again felt great drowsiness, and before she could form another question, she was asleep.

In the morning she was alone in the cave, the embers of the fire cold.

She wondered if she should wait for Quilla to return from wherever she had gone, but the last words she remembered being spoken were still ringing in her head. 'In the morning return to Ma-ii . . . warn everyone to leave the town and to seek sanctuary in the mountains and beyond . . . The days of Ma-ii are over.'

She looked at her wrist. Her seal stone was there. She was Ierii, daughter of Dorran, and she knew that, whether she understood it or not, she was trusted by the Lady Quilla, and must not let her down.

4

The Queen and the Black Bull

When Thyloss reached the palace he found that the princess had indeed been weeping.

Queen Nya-an, as before, received him in her private apartments, and he could see as soon as he entered the room that she was very angry. Her eyes were black fire, and there were two spots of high colour on her cheeks. She dismissed her attendants the instant that he entered, but gestured fiercely to her daughter to stay, although it was clear to Thyloss that the girl would dearly love to leave.

He bowed to the Queen, but looked hard at the princess, seeing things about her that he had not noticed before. Her waist was the slimmest he had ever seen, her breasts almost as flat as a boy's. She could not be more than twelve summers old and yet she was to be given in marriage. She was not ready. He knew it, and she knew it. But the Queen refused to see it.

'It has come to my notice,' the woman now said, her voice trembling with anger, 'that you have allowed the Black Thunderer to be wounded and marked!'

'I did not "allow" it, my lady. It was an accident.'

'Carelessness,' she snapped. 'No excuse whatever.'

'I am not seeking excuse, my lady. It is done and it cannot be undone. I regret it. But he is mending fast and will be ready for the funeral games.'

'He will not be perfect! And I demand perfection for my son.'

Thyloss was silent for a moment.

'Might I suggest another bull, my lady? There are many fine bulls . . .'

'No, you may not suggest another bull. There is no bull on the Island as beautiful, or as potent, as Black Thunderer. It must be he!'

Thyloss bit back what he wanted to say, and was silent.

She gazed at him angrily for a moment or two and then rose from her chair impatiently.

'Take me to him!' she demanded.

Thyloss was astonished. The Queen, who moved nowhere without processions of attendants, and never without giving warning so that her subjects might prepare to greet her with formality, expected him now to take her, like any ordinary woman, to see a sick bull.

'Why do you hesitate?' she said coldly. 'Do you fear that I will see that he is worse than I have been informed?'

'No, of course not, my lady . . . but . . .' Thyloss looked helplessly at the princess. She was watching with round eyes the scene before her, but gave him no indication of what to do next. 'But,' Thyloss continued desperately, 'do you not wish your attendants to accompany you?'

She gave him an amused and haughty look.

'No, I do not wish my attendants to accompany us.'

Thyloss bowed rather clumsily. He was not sure if he should lead the way, or stand back for her. Impatiently she gestured that he should follow her, and she swept out of the room.

He gave a quick look over his shoulder at Meri-an. She gave him a shy and tentative smile. She did not look as unhappy as she had when he arrived. He smiled at her as he turned to follow her mother. He could not think of her as a princess or as his future wife. She was just a child caught, like him, in a situation that was out of her control. It crossed his mind that her name, Meri-an, meant 'daughter of shadow.'

The bull workers, caught off guard, were sitting on the ground playing the age-old game of tannat, using small white pebbles for counters, the board marked out in the dust of the yard. Startled and confused they leapt to their feet. One of them, ever awkward, fell over, sprawling clumsily before the Queen.

Thyloss was amused. It would be a long time before they sat around again playing games when they were supposed to be cleaning out the bull pens.

Surprisingly the Queen took no notice of them, but stalked straight past, making for the chief bull pen.

The Black Thunderer was snorting softly to himself as he munched on the choice food that had been provided. His wounds were healing nicely, but his face was still marred by the swelling of the flesh around his eyes. It was true that he was not going to be at his best for the funeral.

The Queen walked up and down beside the wall and gazed at him from every angle. Thyloss noticed the fierceness had gone out of her face and it was filled with a brooding tenderness that surprised him. What were her thoughts as she gazed at the great black beast? He could not tell.

Her ways and her thoughts were strange to him. He dreaded coming closer under her influence and power as he inevitably must if he was given the 'honours' she had promised him. He did not trust her.

'He will not be ready,' she said softly. 'He will not be a perfect gift.'

She seemed to be talking to herself, and Thyloss wondered if he dared introduce again the subject of another bull.

'He must be ready,' the Queen said suddenly, looking straight at Thyloss. Her gaze was so penetrating it seemed to have the power to create the situation she demanded, against the laws of nature.

'If you would only look at another bull, my lady,' he stammered, but his voice was low and dry, and she did not appear to hear his words. She grasped the bar that held the enclosure gate shut.

Before he or any of the others who were watching could stop her she had lifted it up and walked into the enclosure, dropping the catch behind her.

Thyloss started forward, calling out a warning, but she strode towards the beast without taking any notice of him.

There was pandemonium among the bull workers and the few people who had gathered to see what was going on. Some ran for prods and others for nets. Some children climbed on the wall, chattering with excitement.

Thyloss followed her, cursing her in his heart, but saying nothing aloud lest it should rouse her to some further foolishness.

The Black Thunderer looked up at her approach and rolled his eyes and snorted, but did not move.

She walked steadily forward, woman of black hair and black eyes, holding herself proud and unafraid.

Thyloss kept behind her, but out of sight, ready to spring as only he could, if the black bull attacked.

There was now hardly a sound from the gathered crowd. Some held their hands to their mouths. One woman had covered her eyes. All were locked in a kind of fascinated horror as their queen approached the most dangerous bull Ma-ii had ever known.

And then, strangely, instead of charging at the intruder as the crowd expected, the great animal sniffed at her and together they moved round and round each other in a kind of slow dance.

The woman talked softly to the bull, and the bull seemed to listen.

Thyloss stood, astounded.

The fiery queen was gone . . . soft as silk her voice . . . the dove lady . . . lady of poppies and dreams . . . her voice like distant singing . . .

He had never seen anything like it.

A sigh of awe went through the watching crowd. It was said that she was a goddess? Now there seemed little doubt.

When she finally came out, walking as slowly as she had gone in, every man and woman lifted fist to forehead in a gesture of respect. Thyloss closed the gate behind her and met her eyes. She had a look in them he could not read.

'He will be ready,' she said. 'I make you responsible.'

She did not wait for him to escort her, but left quickly, treading lightly and swiftly the dusty cobbled streets to the palace.

When she was out of earshot everyone started talking at once. The remarkable events of the morning would pass through many versions until they finally took their place in legend.

Thyloss was just wishing that his father were home, when he heard a roar and a scream. The crowd had turned again to the walls to see one of the bull workers being pursued across the enclosure by the Thunderer. Overcome by curiosity to see if the black bull had indeed gone soft, he had climbed over the wall and prodded him. Within moments the great animal was after him, all his old fire and splendour returned. The worker, taken off guard, and not being a trained acrobat, could not move swiftly enough.

The crowd roared to see him lifted by the deadly horns, blood spurting from his side, and roared again to see him flung like a bundle of discarded rags upon the ground, the beast turning to charge again.

Thyloss dashed almost under the hammering hooves to haul the man out, but he could not save him from broken bones and a disfigured face.

'Mother of the Earth! What is the matter with everyone today!' muttered Thyloss, as, dusty and shaken, but unharmed, he fell down on a pile of dry straw to rest in the safety and cool of the storage sheds. Ayan brought him water and news of the gored man, who was being attended to by healers.

'What a fool!' Thyloss kept saying. 'What a cursed fool! He is lucky to be alive.'

'That he is,' Ayan said, 'though his livelihood is gone.'

'Is he so badly wounded?'

'I would say if he walks at all – it will be haltingly.'

Thyloss sighed and shook his head. What more could happen before his father returned? He had been away before, but never had so many things gone wrong.

'I wonder how the Queen did it,' he mused at last.

Ayan pursed his lips disapprovingly.

'You do not like her, do you?' Thyloss said, noticing his expression. He had seen this look on Ayan's face before when the Queen was mentioned.

Ayan did not answer.

'But you must admit – she was magnificent! So unafraid, so bold. She is a remarkable woman. It made me wonder if she was not indeed a goddess as the people think.'

Miron had never taught his son to look upon the Queen as goddess as other fathers had. What he really believed Thyloss did not know, but he made obeisance to nothing and nobody. His own skill and his own strength were what he relied upon. Thyloss loved and respected his father deeply, and had learned from him to hold his mind open, leaning neither to superstition nor to atheism. There were things Miron could not explain about the world, but hoped one day to understand. Meanwhile he taught Thyloss to perfect the skills he had and learn whatever lessons life had to teach.

'She is no goddess,' Ayan said under his breath. 'If anything other than human, she is a demon.'

Thyloss just caught the words and looked startled.

'What makes you say that?'

'Ask your father,' Ayan said, and walked away before he could be questioned further.

Even more intrigued, Thyloss thought about his father. It was odd that the Queen contemplated having such important ceremonies without the presence of Lord Miron, the Keeper of Bulls.

A thought crossed his mind. Was the timing deliberate?

His father would certainly not approve of her plans, and, he had noticed many times, he was the one man who dared stand up to her and refuse her commands.

'There is one who can help us,' Ayan said thoughtfully later, as he and Thyloss stood watching the Thunderer in some despair.

'Who is it? And why have you not mentioned this before?'

'It is a long story,' Ayan said, 'and I was loath to open up old wounds.'

'There is no time for a long story, or for riddles,' Thyloss said impatiently. 'Tell me what I need to know, and swiftly.'

'There is a woman,' old Ayan said, his eyes withdrawn on a memory, 'living in the mountains, a Seer. One who has greater powers than the Queen.'

'I am listening!' Thyloss said sharply, as the old man paused.

'She has been known to heal wounds with the touch of her hand. But . . .'

'But . . . what?'

'I do not know if she would do it now.'

'Why not?'

'She would not approve the Queen's determination to sacrifice the Thunderer at the end of the funeral. She was always against blood sacrifice.'

'Need she know?' Thyloss was ashamed of his thought, but he was tired and desperate.

'She will know,' Ayan said shortly.

Thyloss was silent for a moment. But then he spoke decisively. 'We will ask her help. If she refuses, we have lost nothing. If she accepts, we have gained a great deal.'

'I do not know how to find her,' old Ayan said as though he regretted having mentioned her.

Thyloss had a thought.

'Ierii is in the mountains this very day, seeking a woman she saw in the clouds. She thinks she is the Earth Goddess . . . but . . . could it be . . .'

'It is very possible. The woman I speak of has lived in the mountains as many summers as you have been alive. She has become part of the mountains. She comes and goes as the mist. No one sees her, but many feel her presence.'

'What is her story? Why does she live so?' Thyloss asked with interest.

Ayan looked at him closely, but did not answer.

'Tell me.'

'Nay, I will not tell you, but if you want her help, it is said there is a small grove of trees, halfway up that mountain there.' He pointed. 'If you make offering there, not of bulls, or of axes, but of flowers . . . white lilies and purple irises . . . she will answer your call. She serves the Lady of the Lilies.'

'I will do it,' cried Thyloss. 'Direct me to the place.'

'First you must have the flowers,' Ayan said. .

'I will ask Ierii's father for them.'

'He will give them gladly. He has reason to be grateful to the Goddess. But make sure you have the whole plant, roots as well. Offerings to her must not bring death to any living thing. You must plant the flowers in the sacred grove.'

'How is it that I have not heard of this Seer who serves the Lady of the Lilies before?'

'No one speaks of her.'

'Why?'

'It is someone the Queen banished from the town about the time of your birth. It is forbidden even to mention her name.'

'What is her name?'

Ayan was silent.

'Tell me at least that, my friend, and I will ask no more about her.'

That she served the Lady of the Lilies was enough to cause the Queen, as High Priestess of the Bull Cult, to hate her, but Ayan knew that there was more to the hatred than this. No one would like to be responsible for the Queen discovering her presence so near the town of Ma-ii.

'Some say she is the Lady Quilla.' Ayan's voice was scarcely above a whisper.

Quilla's prowess as an acrobat was almost legendary. But Thyloss had thought that she was dead. He wanted to know more, but Ayan would speak no more about her. He would only give detailed instructions on how to find the grove.

When Thyloss found Dorran he was working in the northern courtyard of the palace. He asked for the lily plants and said that he needed them urgently. But he did not say outright what the purpose was, nor did he mention the forbidden name. The Queen's attendants were close by and Thyloss did not want them carrying information back to her.

Dorran was busy and harassed, but began to understand when Thyloss stressed that it was Ayan who had sent him and that he needed white lilies and purple irises, and that they must not be damaged in any way. Suddenly he straightened his back and looked the boy in the eye.

'You say it is urgent?' he asked searchingly.

'Yes, most urgent.'

The man was thoughtful.

'Did Ayan give you a sign to give to me?'

Thyloss looked puzzled for a moment, thinking back to his last conversation with Ayan.

A sign?

Suddenly he remembered that Ayan had been drawing with a stick in the ground while he had been describing how to find the sacred grove. He had not taken any particular notice at the time, but now a memory of it rose clearly from the depths of his mind.

He stooped down, and in the earth at Dorran's feet, he drew a butterfly. Dorran smiled, and instantly with his foot rubbed out the sketch.

'You shall have the white lilies and the purple irises,' he said with sudden warmth. 'Go to my garden. Take what you need. Be careful to take damp earth with the roots.'

'Thank you,' Thyloss cried, pausing only to press the old man's hand with gratitude before he speeded off.

The mountain Ayan had pointed out to him had been in the ancient days a holy mountain, but of late it had been much neglected. Paths had been worn around it when people had gone on pilgrimages to its summit, spiralling round and round. But these were now mostly overgrown.

Thyloss found one, however, that was in such good condition he could not doubt that it was still in use. He wondered that the Queen's spies had not noticed it. Perhaps they had been told that it was just an herb gatherer's path, for the mountain was redolent with the scent of herbs.

Veins of white crystal were fairly common in the mountains of the Island, but this particular peak seemed to consist almost entirely of white crystal. It was also the mountain over which the full moon rose as spring turned to summer. The mountain was steep and craggy near the top and Thyloss was glad he had to climb no farther than the grove.

Having started from the town so late in the day, he did not reach his destination until the sun was already beginning to stain the sky red, but when he did at last, he caught his breath with the beauty of it.

There were many forests of cedar and of cypress on the Island, but this natural terrace, rich in green and leafy growth, seemed more beautiful than them all. There were trees Thyloss had never seen before growing here, and in the shade and flickering light beneath them, fed by a tiny crystal spring, white lilies and purple irises grew in great profusion. Thyloss thought that if he had not been told about the place, but had stumbled upon it unaware, he would not have failed to feel that it was sacred.

Now, with the approach of evening, as the shadows grew darker and the birds stiller, there was a kind of expectant hush about the place. He could believe that there was someone there who could not be seen with ordinary eyes.

He was not sure how to formulate an appropriate prayer. To request recovery for an animal so that it would be fit enough to be killed, seemed suddenly so monstrous and ridiculous to him that he could not do it.

He found himself, instead, saying nothing in words, but offering himself to the Presence as gift.

He began to feel drowsy and strange, and thoughts swam in his mind like fishes. 'There is some reason why I have been called here. There is some reason for my part in all these strange events. Help me to see it, help me to fulfil it in a way that only good may come of it.'

Sleep overcame him. Sleep that was deeper than the shadows filling the chasms and the crannies of the holy mountain.

When he woke, the moon, almost full, was pouring its light down upon him.

He was refreshed and rested, and rose instantly, remembering the flowers he had brought to plant.

But they were no longer beside him.

The damp, soiled cloth he had carried them in was folded neatly at his feet. The flowers themselves were already in the earth, the deep glow of their petals, and the darkness of their shadows, already part of the magic grove. He felt a tingle of excited awe, and then a very natural shiver as the cool night air touched his skin.

He was not at all sure what had happened, but he was certain that it was time for him to leave. He looked back at the grove as he moved away. He could have sworn it glowed in the moonlight in a way the other trees of the mountain did not.

Whatever the explanation, he thought to himself as he picked his way carefully down the steep path, something had happened out of the ordinary. Something would come of it.

When he reached the town it was sleeping in moon shadow.

He slipped into his house and crept into his bed, and slept better than he had since the day his father went on the hunt and left him with all the responsibilities of the Keeper of the Bulls.

5

The Morning of the Funeral

One morning, at dawn Thyloss was awakened by bustle and noise; shaking his head to free it from the clinging web of sleep, he suddenly realized that this was the day of the funeral, the day his skill and cunning were to be pitted against that of the Black Thunderer and the Queen.

'Thyloss,' somebody called urgently. 'Thyloss!'

He scrambled up, fastening on his short kilt and his sandals almost as he moved across the room. One of the boys who looked after the Thunderer was in the yard, agitated and sweating.

'Come and see,' he was crying. 'Come and see!'

Thyloss followed him at once. Whether it was good or bad news he could not establish from the lad's excited babbling. But when he reached the pen, and pushed past all the people who had gathered around it, he could see that it was good news indeed.

The Black Thunderer was pawing the ground, every mark on his body gone. Thyloss was stunned.

He thought of the Lady Quilla who served the Goddess, but he had not asked her to heal the bull.

Ayan was beside him.

'She did it,' he said with satisfaction.

'But . . .' said Thyloss, bewildered.

'One of the boys saw her,' interrupted Ayan.

'Saw her?'

'Well, very dimly . . . a woman walking into the pen at night . . .'

'Could it have been the Queen?' Thyloss asked suddenly.

Ayan paused. He had not thought of her.

'She has never been known to have healing powers,' he said doubtfully.

'But I never asked for the healing. I felt too ashamed of the reasons.'

'But you found the grove and planted the lilies?'

'I found the grove, but I did not plant the lilies. They sort of . . . planted themselves.' Thyloss' voice trailed away as he thought about the extraordinariness of the whole experience. How would his father explain it all?

Ayan looked impressed.

'She planted the lilies. She heard your prayer.'

'But I did not pray for the Black Thunderer!' Thyloss cried.

'You must be mistaken. The beast is healed.'

Thyloss looked at the animal. He was in perfect shape.

'Has anyone told the Queen?'

'Not yet. We did not want to disturb her so early.'

'1 will tell her,' Thyloss said firmly. 'She made me responsible for him. It is only right that I should tell her.'

Having seen her with the bull the day before, he would not have been completely surprised if she had had something to do with the magic.

But first he must see Ierii.

He went to her home, but the house was deserted. Dorran had left early, and Ierii was not yet returned from the mountains.

Disappointed, he set off for the palace.

The palace, always a busy place, was in turmoil this morning. Servants were running up and down stairs and along the corridors bearing food from the storerooms in the basement to the kitchens. Dorran's team of gardeners was arranging the plants in the galleries around the great court. A group of dancers was practising a new and complicated step the Queen had insisted on introducing into the ceremony. Young girls were scattering drops of scented water to purify the air. Embalmers were clearing away the jars of unguent, the bales of unused linen from the cult rooms, leaving the body of the young prince ready for the ceremony in his honour.

The Queen was nowhere in sight, but the princess was wandering about looking very small and lonely. When she saw Thyloss, her face lit up and she came to him directly.

'I wanted to talk to you,' she said shyly, 'but I did not dare go out of the palace to look for you.'

'I wanted to talk to you too,' he said gently, 'but I have been busy.'

The girl looked rueful.

'I am never busy,' she said sadly. 'I wish I were.'

He smiled.

'Surely you have things to do?'

'Not really. I always seem to be waiting for something to happen, or watching something happen. I am never allowed to take part.'

'What would you like to take part in?' Thyloss asked with curiosity.

The princess looked longingly at the dancers in the corner of the great court, practising their steps.

'I love to dance,' she said shyly. 'But I am never allowed.'

Everyone danced on the Island. How sad to be a princess and not allowed to dance!

'Come with me,' he said. 'I will ask them if you can join them.'

'Oh no!' She flushed. 'My mother will be angry.'

'I am sure she will not,' he said firmly, taking her arm like an elder brother, forgetting that she was to be queen one day and possibly his wife. Her eyes shone with a mixture of joy and fear.

The dancers were a little disconcerted at first to have the princess join them, but Thyloss persuaded them to show her the steps. At first when she joined arms with them she could not feel the rhythm of the music inside her in the way they seemed to, and her movements were out of harmony with theirs.

Thyloss broke into the circle, put his hand on her shoulder, and gently guided her. Within moments she became an indistinguishable part of the circle of moving figures. Thyloss slipped away, giving her an encouraging smile, pleased to see her looking so happy. The whole question of his marriage to this child seemed so unreal he could not let it worry him. There was so much else to be endured before then.

The Queen stood beside her son where the embalmers had left him lying in state. The room opened onto the west side of the great central courtyard, where some of the ceremonies would take place.

After the banquet the guests would file past him to pay their respects and then go on to the galleries overlooking the court to watch the dancing.

How calm and beautiful he seemed. The gold mask that now covered his face gave him a look of dormant power. The lines of the mouth were firm and strong; the eyes of lapis lazuli, fathomless.

Was this the son who had caused her so much pain? She had loved him to distraction and he had been taken from her.

So be it. He would come again as king and god.

'My lord!' She bowed to his still figure. 'You will be pleased with your humble servant . . .'

So engrossed was she that she did not notice the youth Thyloss standing at the entrance to the chamber, watching the scene, fascinated. She was in her robes as priest-goddess, flounce upon flounce of skirt edged with gold, apron of gold, breasts bare with nipples cased in gold, and gold upon her neck and arms and hair . . . snakes of gold . . . the snakes of death . . . the snakes of knowledge . . .

But her bearing to her son was humble.

Thyloss began to realize she really believed the dead boy

was being transformed into some supernatural and all powerful deity.

'The bull you asked for waits for you,' she said to the embalmed figure. 'He is perfect once again. I offered a sacrifice to my lord and my lord gave me the gift of his wholeness.'

Thyloss frowned. What sacrifice?

He took a step forward.

The Queen swung around, her eyes blazing in anger that anyone would dare intrude upon her private communion with the dead prince.

For a moment Thyloss trembled at the coldness of her gaze . . . and then the lady smiled.

'Come, Thyloss,' she said softly. 'You shall be the first to greet our new god.'

He looked at the dead prince and hesitated.

'Come!' she commanded, a sharp edge to her voice.

He stepped forward, but did not raise his arm in respect as she expected. Fire flickered in her eyes, but she restrained herself.

'You wait for the ceremony, I see. Well, that is your decision. I hope my lord will not remember it against you.'

Thyloss knew that she was not speaking of the king, her husband, but of the macabre figure of gold and bone lying before them.

He thought how strange it was that names chosen at birth often had significance later. The kindly, self-effacing king, consort of the formidable queen of Ma-ii, had been named Ma-ii-nal, 'servant of Ma-ii.' the prince had been given the name Kel-urr, 'the shining one.' In his life it was inappropriate. In death, he was cased in gold.

'My lady,' Thyloss said, lifting his chin proudly and looking her in the eye. 'You spoke of the Black Thunderer and you mentioned a sacrifice. What sacrifice?'

She smiled knowingly and turned to walk across the room, her skirts swishing as she moved.

'That is between me and my lord.' she said.

Thyloss felt his muscles tautening with the effort to control himself. He wanted to shake the words out of her.

'If I am to be your son . . .' he said at last, his voice painstakingly calm, 'should we not avoid secrets between us?'

She turned on him and her face was white with rage.

'You presume too much, youth! You are not my equal, nor ever will be! What secrets I have, I keep . . . but may the Dark Lord smite you if ever you dare to keep anything from me!'

Thyloss swallowed and was silent, but he did not lower his eyes.

After a moment of tenseness their eyes parted; the Queen changed her mood and Thyloss relaxed a little.

'You have come to tell me that the Black Thunderer is completely recovered?' she asked.

'Yes, my lady,' Thyloss said.

'Do you know how it happened?' she added, her eyes challenging and mocking, but her voice as smooth as silk.

'N-no,' he answered, with a slight hesitation.

'But you think I had something to do with it?'

'I heard you say so, my lady.'

She laughed.

'Who else?' she said with satisfaction.

He did not reply, but his face showed that he was thinking of someone else.

'Who else?' she screamed, her mood changing as suddenly as it had changed before.

'No one, my lady!' he stammered, having enough sense not to mention the Lady of the Lilies, or her banished handmaiden.

'You are thinking of someone else!'

'No. No,' he protested.

She stood before him, willing him with her black gaze to give up his thoughts, but, although priestesses had many unusual skills, and as Queen she was also high priestess of the Bull Cult, her anger prevented her making full use of them. He gave her no help but lowered his eyes and thought about the black bull and only the black bull.

What would have happened next had the king, her husband, not come into the chambers, Thyloss would never know. He could not remember ever having been so pleased to see anyone.

'My lord!' He bowed at once and started to retreat.

'No, stay,' said the king kindly. 'My lady, Nya-an, tells me that you are to marry our daughter, Meri-an.'

Thyloss stood helpless. This was another subject that had difficulties for him.

'I am pleased,' the king said mildly. 'She is a nice child and deserves a good husband.'

Thyloss warmed to him. How different he was from his wife, and how different was his attitude toward their daughter.

'Thank you, my lord,' Thyloss said softly, bowing in respect to the kindliness and gentleness of the king. 'But if you will excuse me, I must go and prepare for the Funeral challenge.'

And then, without a glance at the Queen, and before she could say a word, he bowed again and left.

Some distance from Ma-ii, during the night that Thyloss took the lilies as an offering to the Lady upon the mountain, and Ierii slept in the cave, Miron dreamed of Quilla so vividly he woke with a start, sure that she was with him.

But, awake, he could not see her.

Miron and his men had erected a temporary pen of wooden stakes to hold the fierce white bull they had captured, and he could hear it pawing and snorting, angered at its unaccustomed confinement.

The others were sleeping on the hard ground, soundly, after the day's exertions, occasional snores from them contributing to the restless sounds of the night.

Wide awake and disturbed by old memories, he rose and relieved the boy on watch. There was still some time before they had to move, though first light was beginning to creep over the sky from the east, and he could hear at least one bird sing. He sat on the stump of an old tree that had been felled by lightning and watched the captive bull. As though aware of the man's thoughts, the beast grew calm and came to the edge of the pen to stare at him through the bars.

Miron had not seen Quilla since she had disappeared just before their son Thyloss had been born. He was younger than her, and yet the father of her son Thyloss.

He himself had been born the youngest son of the previous Keeper of the Queen's Bulls, yet, as a child, he had felt that he was nobody. His elder brothers and sisters outshone him in everything and seemed always to take his parents' attention away from him. As a youth watching Quilla dance with the bulls had become an obsession with him. He followed her every move, worshipping her. As a young man he took courage to speak with her and gradually, from talk about the finer points of bull dancing, their communication widened to everything that concerned them and finally blossomed into love.

It was her love for him that transformed him from gauche youth to confident man and it was with her help he proved himself to his father and was finally appointed to succeed him as Keeper of the Queen's Bulls.

At the ceremony in which he took responsibility for his new office, the Queen Nya-an saw him. Conscious of nothing but his and Quilla's joy in his appointment he did not notice the look in the young queen's dark eyes and, when he was called to her private apartments, he went innocently and willingly. It was only when she dismissed her attendants and drew aside the curtain to her bedchamber that he suddenly realized what kind of predicament he was in.

Quietly, politely, he refused her, telling her of his love for the Lady Quilla and that she carried his child. He should have been warned by the dark fire in her eyes, but he was not.

Quilla disappeared.

He accused the Queen of having something to do with her disappearance and demanded to know where she was. But she only laughed, saying: 'She grew tired of you!'

And that is what many said.

He never saw Quilla again but at the next full moon a newly born baby boy was found at the foot of his bed, Quilla's seal stone bound upon his wrist, the device upon it, lilies carved in agate. He called his son 'Thyloss', meaning 'child of the lily'.

For a long time he searched for her, following every rumour that was breathed about women answering her description seen in various parts of the Island. He searched the mountains for the Seer who was rumoured to live there, waited night after night in the sacred grove, but never once did he find a trace of her. He persuaded himself that she had left the country altogether and gone perhaps to Egypt where he knew she had spent some time when she was young.

His son needed looking after and eventually he married his widowed cousin Mahra, whom he liked but did not love. She had nothing of Quilla's quicksilver beauty and deep mystical wisdom, but she had a kind, warm heart and an understanding of their relationship. With gentle, persistent care, she raised Quilla's fiery son with her own children and those she and Miron later had together.

Miron's reverie was suddenly interrupted by the snort of the bull in its makeshift pen. It had begun to pace up and down in the agitated way a caged animal does when it senses something unusual and possibly alarming.

Miron looked at it puzzled and then spun round as he himself heard a movement behind him.

Faintly luminous, the figure of Quilla stood before him.

'No, you are not dreaming,' she answered his thought. 'But neither are you fully awake. No!' She held up her hand as he prepared to move towards her. 'Do not come to me. I am not with you in the sense we both long for.'

He had known that she could spirit-travel, but had never seen her do so and, in fact had not really believed her when she had told him about it. He wanted to speak but his longing for her choked the words in his throat.

'We have no time now for talk, my love, of what was, or what might have been. I left you because I had to, not because I wanted to.'

His eyes told her that he needed more than that.

'Nya-an promised death to you and our child if I stayed, success and fame for both of you if I left'

'What was success and fame without you!' At last the words burst out, painfully, angrily.

'Trust me,' she said sadly. 'It was not as simple as that. You know as well as I that we are not simple game pieces on a board. It was not just the Queen who spoke to me that day, but the Spirit-realms and my own intuition. I knew that from that point on the three of us, you, me and our child, had separate destinies, just as I know today that our coming together is for some purpose greater than ourselves . . .'

He tried to hold the bitterness and the yearning down. He had lived long enough to know that what she said had truth in it, though he resented it.

'But why now?' he said at last huskily. 'Why is it now that you come to me?'

'I need you,' she said. 'Thyloss needs you. Ma-ii needs you.'

'And what of my needs?' his heart cried.

The last rays of the moonlight played on her figure so that it looked transparent: the air shimmered around her.

'Stay!' he cried aloud. 'Be with me a while longer. Tell me where I may find you!'

'You will find me . . .'

Her voice faded . . . her shape dissolved in light.

Miron gave a cry that was so full of pain and longing it sounded like something from the wild places of the hills.

Some of his men stirred and woke. They saw their master with a stick in his hand and his eyes distraught, pushing the bushes aside, searching wildly for something.

'My lord!' Giro cried. 'What is it?' He leapt up with spear and dagger ready, convinced that some savage beast was threatening them.

Miron paused and looked at him, startled. He had forgotten where he was, and who he was. He had remembered only his love for Quilla. Pulling himself together he said sharply: 'It was a mountain lion. It must have scented the bull.'

They looked around them uneasily. The strong half-light of early dawn was still full of shadows.

Later when the hunters were preparing their food, Miron startled them again with his restlessness and impatience. Something had made him want to return to Ma-ii quickly, and they were hurried unmercifully until they were on their way without taking as much care as usual to leave no mess behind them. Most of the stakes were still left in the ground; only those were taken that were easy to remove.

They were at least a full day's travel from Ma-ii, but Miron was determined to make it less. Quilla would not have appeared for nothing.

There had been many dangers in the years since she had left, and not once had she appeared to warn him of them.

A frown was on his brow and his men could get nothing out of him. Oppressed by the mood he was in, they went about their tasks silently and morosely; only the strange whistling calls of the drovers broke the air around them as they moved.

Halfway through the morning they were startled to feel a vibration in the earth. The bull felt it first and its agitated lowing brought them to a halt.

'Stupid beast,' Giro had muttered bad-temperedly, tired by the pace they had been travelling at and the unusual oppression of spirit caused by Miron's mood, when he felt the tremor too, and his horrified eyes met those of his master.

It was not large or definite enough for them to be sure it was the forerunner of an earthquake, but it was enough to bring fear to their hearts. A low grumbling growl seemed to come from the earth beneath them, and one or two small rocks fell off the hillside near them and scattered into the valley.

Miron called them together and they did their best to calm the animal, though it heaved on its ropes mightily.

The tremor was soon over and they tried to tell themselves they had imagined it. But they knew that they had not.

After that Miron did not need to drive them with his own strong will. They were all determined to return to their families as quickly as possible in spite of the gruelling heat of the day. On the Island of the Bulls the moving of the earth was feared greatly. Had not whole cities been destroyed in ancient times? The palaces themselves were built upon the ruins of others.

Thyloss had left the palace and was on his way to check that all the arrangements for the funeral games on the Field of Challenge were complete when he met Ierii hurrying down the Street of the Dolphin.

'Thyloss!' she cried. 'I have been searching everywhere for you. Where have you been?'

The youth's face lit up when he saw her, but he did not stop walking.

'Ierii! Come with me. I have no time to stop, but there is a great deal I have to tell you.'

She almost had to run to keep up with his easy, swinging stride, but she did so with pleasure.

'I saw the Lady,' she cried, 'and . . .'

'I went to the mountain myself,' he interrupted, 'to the sacred grove, and the Black Thunderer was miraculously healed . . .'

'She is not the Goddess,' Ierii tried to say, 'but she is . . .'

'The others think it was the Queen healed the Black Thunderer and she thinks that herself . . . but I am sure it was the Goddess or at least the Seer. The white lilies and the irises were planted while I was asleep and, Ierii, I am sure it was no ordinary sleep . . .'

'I slept too – and I too am sure it was no ordinary sleep. Thyloss . . .'

But he still would not listen.

'The Queen has done something . . . she talked of a sacrifice that had already been made. I found her talking to her son as though he were a god and she wanted me to accept him as a god too. She is mad I think. She is obsessed by that son of hers . . .'

'Thyloss!' Ierii suddenly shouted and pulled at his arm.

Surprised, he stopped walking and looked at her. He had never known her make such a loud and angry sound.

'You will listen to me. You will!' she said fiercely.

Then he apologized. 'I thought you would want to know what has been going on,' he said.

'Of course I do – but there are things you must know too. I must tell you. I must!'

'All right,' he said. They had reached the market place and he stooped to drink from the water that spouted from the stone mouth of the dolphin that guarded the spring, the dolphin that was originally placed there to remind the people of Ma-ii that their lives, though as brief as a dolphin's leap, returned always to the great ocean of Spirit from which they came. 'Tell me,' Thyloss said, cupping his hands for the cool clear water.

'She is not the Goddess,' Ierii said, 'though she serves her. Thyloss, she is beautiful, wonderful . . . I understood so many things when I was with her . . .'

'Did you tell her about today . . . what the Queen is planning?'

'Yes, but Thyloss . . . she said . . . she said . . .'

Ierii's heart was beating fast. She was determined to tell Thyloss what she had learned, but she was afraid.

Thyloss poured the water over his head and shook his long hair.

'What did she say?'

'She said,' and here Ierii took a deep breath and brought the next words out in a rush. 'She said you were her son and that she and Miron had . . .'

Thyloss straightened up at once and looked at her, startled.

'What are you saying?'

'I know it seems impossible . . . but she told me a great deal about the Queen and . . . and your father . . . and how she and your father had been lovers and the Queen had made her go away when you were born and now the Queen is probably giving you all those honours because . . .'

Just at this moment, when Thyloss was staring at her in astonishment, the earth tremor that Miron had felt in the mountains shook the ground under their feet. Ierii screamed and flung herself into his arms. Involuntarily he held her close, his mind in turmoil with all that was happening and all that was being revealed. It seemed a hundred years ago that he had been peacefully practising for the funeral games, never dreaming that he was to be the challenger. And now . . .

A wall he could see over Ierii's head was beginning to crack and sway. Instinctively he pulled her out of reach of it if it should fall. But the tremor was already over, and the wall did not fall.

Ierii lifted her head and looked at him anxiously. He was frowning. At the back of his mind he was remembering the earth tremor and thinking that this would justify the Queen's sacrifice of the Black Thunderer in the eyes of the people. It would be natural for them to sacrifice a bull to the Dark Lord of Destruction on the day the earth had shaken. But he was also thinking of his father and the mother that he knew, and the strange Lady on the mountain who claimed to be his mother

'She said all sorts of things Thyloss. The hardest to understand – I mean after what she said about you – was that I was to tell the people that the days of Ma-ii were over and that they must flee to the mountains and – "beyond".' She paused. All the way back from the mountain Ierii had been worrying about this task Quilla had set her. How could she tell them? Who would listen to her? But now after the earth had trembled might they not listen? Might they not follow her to the mountains and 'beyond'?

There was a plateau behind the mountains, a fertile plain

cupped between peaks.[1] She had heard tell of it, but had never been there.

Was this where Quilla intended them to go?

She became miserably afraid, and wished that everything could continue as it had always done. The quiet round of the days in Ma-ii had been pleasant and untroubled. Could they not be so again?

'What are we to do, Thyloss?' she asked sadly. 'What are we to do?'

He was silent and thoughtful.

The time for the first of the ceremonies was approaching fast. The first of the important guests were already arriving at the palace and soon there would be the banquet, then the dancing, then the challenge of the dark god. Death would be mocked. Death would be conquered. The body of the young Prince Kel-urr would be carried in processional triumph to his tomb near the sea.

'Thyloss . . .' Ierii's voice broke into his thoughts.

He looked at her. Her dark eyes were looking into his as though she wished she could become part of his very soul and feel no more the pain of separation. Strangely, this time he felt no irritation with the intensity of her love, but felt a response almost equally intense within himself. They now shared secret knowledge that cut them off from the rest of the town. They shared a responsibility that no one else knew about. He suddenly realized that he trusted her more than anyone he had ever known.

'Ierii,' he said, 'so many strange things have happened to us we must believe they have some meaning, even if we do not know what that meaning is. We will warn the people as the Lady Quilla told us to. We will speak openly of the Lady of the Lilies.'

'And against the sacrifice?' added Ierii eagerly.

Thyloss had not always shared her revulsion against sacrifice in general. He had accepted it as part of tradition, and had never questioned it. But this new twist to the ancient ritual troubled him.

'And against the sacrifice!' he said at last, with conviction, although he knew this would bring the Queen's wrath down upon his head.

On the mountain, in the moonlight, he had glimpsed within himself levels that he did not know he had. He thought impatiently about the funeral and all the difficulties of the day. He would like time to think about what he had glimpsed. He would like time to think about what Ierii had told him about his mother.

'There is not time,' she said gloomily, as though she had read his thoughts.

'There is time,' a voice said softly behind them.

They spun round.

The beautiful Lady Quilla, Thyloss' mother, stood before them.

She was looking at them both with great love.

'Awareness is outside time. You can "know" the splendour of the universe in less time than it takes you to blink an eye.'

She lifted her hand suddenly, and it seemed as though everything in the busy world stood still.

Between the drawing and the expulsion of a breath there was a hiatus, and Ierii and Thyloss experienced awareness of such subtle complexity that they understood why they existed, knew that they had always existed and would always exist. They knew that there was nothing in the shining forest of space and time that was not rooted in the centre of all consciousness, and did not draw its life from there.

Quilla dropped her hand.

Ierii blinked and gasped.

Thyloss rubbed his eyes.

They were both shaken, dazed, finding everything around them the same, and yet nothing was the same.

Quilla smiled.

'You see?'

No time had passed, and yet the experience had seemed to take up more time than they had ever known.

'You have done your thinking, and now it is time to act,' Quilla said, drawing them back to the moment with a voice that was gentle, but commanding.

'But what must we do?' Ierii asked, bewildered.

'Think. Draw on what you have just learned.'

Ierii and Thyloss looked at each other.

When they turned to look back at Quilla, she was no longer there.

'We are on our own,' Ierii said sadly.

Thyloss took her hand and held it fast. There seemed no words to be said.

A few moments later they had to part. Thyloss was called to the Field of Challenge, and Ierii remembered that she was expected to be present at the funeral banquet.

At noon the feast in the great banqueting hall began.

Since the weather was warm with the approach of summer, the screens were drawn back and the air circulated freely. The view of the sea to the north and the eastern part of the great arc of mountains that held Ma-ii in its arms was breathtaking.

The court and all its guests were in their best finery. A funeral on the Island was never a gloomy occasion. Whatever the personal feelings of the bereaved might be, the general mood was one of celebration. Death meant parting, it is true, but only to start life again in another form.

Prince Kel-urr, according to the Queen, was at this very moment taking his rightful place as one of the 'gods', one of the spirit guardians of the powerful forces of the universe. In the future the people would turn to him if they needed help. To him they would make sacrifices if they were afraid.

The Queen had been jubilant when she had felt the earth tremble during the morning.

'You see!' she had cried. 'My son is impatient for his steed!'

Her ladies had looked uneasily at each other. They were in awe of the Queen, but hoped desperately that she was wrong about her son. She had doted on him, a boy no one else could bear. He was mean and spiteful. His private games always involved torturing little animals or insects. His own sister had many a scar to show for his 'playfulness'. They were terrified to think of him wielding supernatural powers.

Princess Meri-an, who should have been the one to receive the most attention, being, as only daughter, heir to the throne, had been treated all her life like some minor court official's daughter, expected to wait upon her mother but given no love or trust in return.

There had been talk that the Queen might even reverse the ancient tradition of female succession and appoint her son to reign after her death instead of her daughter. They had been spared that by the boy's death. Now they were not sure if it would not have been the lesser of two evils. The thought of the sadistic prince as god in control of even some of the earth's destructive forces was not a comforting one.

The scene in the banqueting hall was one of great splendour. The table at which Ierii was sitting consisted of thin slabs of alabaster fitted cunningly together on a frame of fine cedar wood. Cups of crystal and papyrus-thin pottery stood upon its almost transparent surface. Fruit stands, balanced on slender columns and painted with flowers and leaves, rose above bowls of spiced meat and sugared sweetmeats. Tall vases held scarlet blooms. Small rounded copper dishes shone beneath the vine leaves that trailed from them.

The guests themselves were magnificent, each one apparently trying to vie with his neighbour in elegance of dress. The women were in the traditional costume expected of court ladies, layer upon layer of skirts of differing lengths over stiff linen petticoats. Their bodices were cut low and the white powdered skin of their necks and breasts was gleaming with many necklaces. Ierii herself wore her mother's beads of alternate purple amethyst and transparent rock crystal.

The Princess Meri-an was dressed in fine pleated white

Egyptian cotton, a single gold pendant on her thin neck, two hornets exquisitely worked by the goldsmith, holding between them a honeycomb in the shape of the sun. Ierii noticed that the simple tastefulness of the young girl's appearance made many of the women appear ornate and vulgar. She was glad she had not borrowed some grander clothes than her own from the friend who had offered them.

The men, their tanned skins made darker for the occasion with special oils and powders, wore long, unpleated kilts of linen, bordered and embroidered in some cases with threads of another colour, sometimes of silver and of gold. Above the waist they were naked except for the necklaces around their throats and the elaborate coronets of jewels, flowers, and feathers in their long hair.

Ierii's father had no tall and fancy headpiece, but a thin silver band bound his grey hair close to his head, and one white lily was tucked almost unseen into the back of it, at the nape of his neck. He wore no necklaces and his kilt was plain, the colour of leaves in spring.

Ierii sat quietly beside Dorran, her heart beating fast with anxiety, knowing that sooner or later she must take advantage of the fact that all the important people of Ma-ii were gathered here, and she would have to stand up and make herself heard among them. The Lady Quilla's message had to be delivered.

She could sense, above her own unease, the tension of the court. For all the bright talk and laughter, most of the guests were very well aware that something unusual and disturbing was about to take place. The earth tremor had made them nervous enough and now the Queen's own behaviour was worrying them further. Her eyes were fever-bright. From her expression and the jerky movements of her hands as she reached for her food and wine, it seemed as though she were holding back the violence of her nature with great difficulty.

As the young serving men passed from guest to guest with the crystal jars of wine, the babble of voices grew louder and louder, the laughter wilder and wilder.

Ierii began to feel very hot; beads of sweat broke out on her forehead. If only Thyloss were with her! But he was preparing to challenge the Black Thunderer, and she would have to speak the Lady Quilla's words alone.

She was just thinking with relief that it would not be her fault if she did not deliver the warning, for the talk around the table was too loud for her voice to be heard, when the arrival of a long line of beautiful young boys and girls, each bearing a dish of the most extravagant delicacies decorated with peacock feathers, caused the guests to gasp and be silent.

The Queen watched with satisfaction as they circled around the guests so that all could see the artistry of the cooks.

When they began to set the dishes down, Ierii, flushed crimson, rose and knocked over a delicate crystal goblet as she did so.

The crash brought all eyes to her.

To Ierii the whole hall full of people seemed to retreat behind an unreal and dream-like haze. She could hear her voice, unusually strained, coming out of her throat and going among them, but she was not aware of herself willing it to do so.

The voice said, 'My lady, my lord . . . and all who are of Ma-ii . . . I have to warn you . . . I mean . . . I have a warning . . .'

Ierii was half aware of the terrible silence around her . . . of the attention she was commanding. She trembled, but she carried on.

'I have been told to tell you that Ma-ii is . . . finished. Its time is over. We must all leave . . . before it is buried under the earth, under the sea . . .'

'Sit down, girl!' thundered the Queen. 'The child is drunk! Dorran look to her.'

'No . . . no, my lady,' cried Ierii. 'You must listen. You heard the earth tremble today. The Lady Quilla says . . .'

'Silence!'

The royal command was terrible and fierce.

Ierii was silent.

She was shivering so much she thought she would fall down. Her father put his arm around her.

Softly he whispered to her.

'Quiet, my girl . . . quiet, my little dove . . . it is no use . . . no one will listen.'

The Queen stood up and looked around her guests. Her face was black as a storm before it breaks.

She pointed a finger like a sword at Ierii's heart.

'You all heard her!' she almost screamed. 'You heard the name she spoke! The name that it is forbidden to speak! Take her away! Never let me see her again.'

In the shocked silence no one moved.

'Now!' screamed the Queen.

Ierii's father stood up and took his daughter from the hall. She was trembling and weeping.

'I had to warn them . . .' she sobbed.

The Queen stood stiff and straight watching her go. Her eyes were dark with bitter memories.

Those around her were silent and nervous. They all knew that it was the name of Quilla that had upset her and distracted her from the young girl's warning. But there were some among them who had great respect for the Lady Quilla, and her warning made them cold with fear.

She was a Seer, in touch with the Spirit Realms and with the earth forces. If energies were beginning to move for the destruction of Ma-ii, Quilla would know of them.

They began to shift uneasily in their seats and wondered if it were possible to leave the funeral feast to gather their belongings and flee from the doomed town. But looking at the Queen's fierce face, they knew that they did not dare.

6

The Seven Prayers of the Seer

At the time Ierii spoke her name before the Queen, Quilla was in the sacred grove on the holy mountain. She had carefully laid out the pattern of a maze beneath the trees with small white stones. She had based her pattern on the sacred number seven and to walk it she passed the centre seven times before she reached it. The constant turning and bending of the path meant that at the end she had covered a great distance and yet never moved farther than a few metres from where she had started.

This type of maze had always been associated with the Goddess.[2] It was inspired by the spiral, one of the most basic and evocative symbols in nature, and there was no question of getting lost within it. The path had no branches into which one was tempted. There was only one possible way to go and that way led to the centre and out again. In the Cult of the Goddess it was used as a means to find the True Self. It was a way of slowing down from the busy rush of everyday life, of moving in an orderly progression, taking each step as one became ready for it, until the centre was reached which was at once the centre of the maze and the sensitive point of consciousness from which all Being springs.

From the stillness at the central point the pilgrim wound slowly outwards again to the exit which was, at the same time, the entrance. On reaching this he or she was ready to face whatever there was to face with a greater inner strength and calmness.

The Bull Cult had its own maze, but it was of the oppo-

site type. It was deliberately designed to confuse and to fos-
ter fear. Within its cruel pattern one could wander helplessly,
taking wrong turn after wrong turn down side alleys which
led nowhere. It was a challenge and those who did not per-
ish in it and found their way out, emerged either aggressively
elated and ready to command the world, or crushed in spirit
and ready to be commanded.

At the centre of Quilla's maze, for extra strength, she had
laid seven crystals. These she had chosen carefully from the
most holy part of the mountain, the summit, where they had
lain exposed to the sun and the moon and the stars for more
centuries than she could count.

She had held them in her hands during meditation and
charged them with the inner strength she then had.

She knew only too well how frail the human will is, how
easily it wavers and leaves its course when difficulties arise,
and she had learned long ago, as many had before her, that
there were times when she would need help to move from
one level of reality to another, to the other realms that are
always with us, shaping our lives, and yet inaccessible to
our ordinary senses.

Even she, Seer and anchorite, had moments when she
found it difficult to control her physical mind and emotions.
At such moments a talisman, a relic of someone who had
more strength than she, or even just something she had held
at a moment of great insight, could remind her of how to
make the passage from one reality to another.

Now, as she walked through the maze on the day of the
prince's funeral, she knew that this was a time she needed help.
Her heart was agitated. Her love for Miron and for Thyloss,
and now her affection for the girl Ierii, was disturbing her. She
feared the suffering that was coming and longed to avert it,
forgetting for the moment that whatever happens on one plane
is only a part of a much greater experience happening on many
other planes to the spirit travelling through eternity.

She found at first that she could not tune to the inner
harmony of the wisdom that she needed, but as she walked

the slow and turning path between the quiet stones, she found her anxiety becoming less, her heart calmer. She began to speak the seven prayers that she had learned when she became a Seer.

From seven sources she gleaned her knowledge, each prayer releasing a different wisdom.

'Speak, trees, and I will listen.'

Roots reach deep into the earth and draw on earth knowledge and earth mystery. Branches reach to the sky and are familiar with air knowledge and air mystery.

'Speak, rock, and I will listen.'

The natural rock of the mountain holds impressions long and gives its knowledge in deep and subtle ways.

Rock moves and flows and changes through time like clouds blowing in the wind. Only the pace is different. There was not the smallest piece of the vast mountain of stone that rose so majestically above the plains of Ma-ii that had not passed through many forms . . . molten and fiery . . . cold and hard . . . cracked, broken, chiselled by frost and water . . . fallen into sand . . . blown by wind . . . stacked and layered . . . hardening yet again . . .

Quilla knew how to feel the pulse of rock, knew when some restless urge would make it stir.

'Speak, dreams, and I will listen.'

Spirit speaks in symbols which are like seeds, releasing wisdom gradually with growth.

Symbols are given in dreams.

Lately Quilla had experienced a restlessness in her dreams. Beside her as she walked she felt the presence of darkness, but when she turned to confront it, it was gone. She had thought at first that it was the shadow of her own death.

But death was not darkness to her. So familiar was she with different realms of being that she had no doubt that there were others still to be explored and that death would be the entrance to them.

No, this was something else.

She began to have recurring nightmares of the earth split-

ting open . . . the sky on fire . . . the sea boiling and rising
. . . rising

'Speak, Silence, and I will listen.'

In silence she could hear the hum of the universe, the infinite harmony of separate sounds that made up the perfection of the one ultimate silence.

She knew nothing happened by accident, separate from everything else.

That Ierii and Thyloss should cross her path at this time had meaning.

Her long sojourn on the mountain, cut off from all that had given her such pleasure in her youth, had meaning.

She knew that without those long, slow years of learning the skills of prophecy, she would not have been able to play the role she now was called upon to play.

The training of a Seer is the training of a human who wants to reach higher than any other human, see further, understand more deeply.

There were times when she had longed for the jarring noise and bustle of the town, the adulation of the crowds as she pitted her physical skill against that of the bull, the warmth of Miron's embrace, her son's kiss. But the Queen had sworn to destroy Miron and her son if she stayed with them. She had been promised that if she left them they would be helped in every way.

The night had been dark indeed when Quilla had had to make this decision; she might very well have decided to stay in defiance of the Queen, or to take her loved ones away from the Island (for nowhere in this land did the jealous queen's wrath not reach), had she not gone to the mountains and listened to the voice of Silence.

As a young woman she had fallen under the influence of a foreign priest, a young man from the land of Egypt, one of the most powerful kingdoms in the world. His name was Khu-ren and he had spoken to her of a secret sect to which he belonged, the Lords of the Sun. She had joined the sect and been trained in its mysteries.[3]

The Lords of the Sun had perfected a way of travelling in spirit-form, which made it possible for them to link up with others of their sect across the world. In every country, no matter what the differences of culture, they found people who were tuned to their vibration, and could help them to use the inner depths of understanding that they had not before been aware of. They taught that there was no limit to what man could do if he harmonized with the flow of energy from the Ultimate Source.

Through her experiences as one of the Lords of the Sun she learned much, but on the holy mountain on the night of her great decision, she learned that it was not enough.

Her brilliant and daring life as an acrobat, her deeply interesting life during the time she was with the Lords of the Sun, even the satisfying warmth of her love for Miron, were important in themselves, but they only led up to one more thing that would be asked of her before she rejoined the Spirit Realms and found another form for her Being.

'Speak, Light, and I will listen.'

Miron and she had been together and loved each other, but there was a time they had to be parted, and she knew that the Queen's jealousy was not the only reason for their parting. That which is beyond this life had separated them for reasons of its own, and now might be bringing them back together.

Since the time of their parting, she had never returned to the town except to lay their son at the feet of Miron.

She knew that it was cowardly not to say goodbye to him, to explain . . . but she knew that if Miron had held her in his arms once more she would not have been able to leave, nor to obey the shining Beings of Light that she had encountered on the holy mountain.

She believed that there was something of great importance she had to do, something for which she was being trained.

Around her the trees of the grove dissolved in light and she was floating in light. The fifth turn of the maze took her to the heart of Light. With its power she saw the beauty of the Spirit Realms . . . the luminous form of the Lady drifting among white lilies . . .

'Speak, Eternity, and I will listen.'

Time could not speak, for it had no voice.

Quilla saw it for what it was . . . yet another tableau man had invented to facilitate his life in this world. Beyond this world, past, present and future are simultaneous, their separation an illusion, all three present in the action of any given moment. Eternity is a state of Being untouched by Time, a quality, rather than a quantity.

Words came to her but she could not grasp them until she clothed them in the myths of her people. She visualized the Bull God, the Dark Lord, the Destroyer taking with force and passion the Lady of the Lilies, Goddess of life and growth, and from their union the earth with all its rich variety being created. This was at once a picture of what had 'happened' in the remote past and what was 'happening' at this moment. The energy of Life being always the moment of strike between the forces of destruction and the forces of creation.

She understood at last that to deny the Destroyer was to deny life. The Lady by herself could not give birth. Life depended on the fusion of the two opposing forces by the mysterious, violent, beautiful energy of Love. The mountain she was walking on, the city below her, were to be destroyed – but this had to be accepted for it was an essential part of life and renewal. While we have the illusion of Time we fear the earthquake and the consuming fire. When we are in pure spirit form we experience Eternity, and fear nothing.

At the centre of the maze she spoke the prayer that was the seventh.

'Speak, Understanding, and I will listen.'

She no longer feared the cataclysm she could sense approaching. It was not so much that she understood it, but that she suddenly felt great relief and joy – an inexpressible feeling that everything, the earthquake and the opening seed, were present simultaneously in her heart as one experience – not two.

The leaves of the trees around her sang in the wind . . .

7

Grey Wind

It was not until noon and the guests were all at the banquet that Thyloss learned the nature of the Queen's sacrifice.

In the morning so much attention had been paid to the Black Thunderer's miraculous recovery that no one had noticed that Grey Wind was missing. But about the time Ierii was making her attempt to warn the Queen and her guests about the destruction of Ma-ii, some children came running into the bull quarters with news that they had seen a terrible sight. So frantic and incoherent were they that it was not until Thyloss and the others had followed them to the south pasture that they understood what had happened.

The carcase of Grey Wind was lying on its side, innumerable scavenging birds tearing at its flesh, a bronze double axe embedded neatly in its skull.

'Mother of the Earth!' Thyloss muttered, staring at the sight.

At their approach the birds had flown up and were sitting on neighbouring trees screeching impatiently.

That the bull had been killed as a sacrifice was obvious from the position of the double axe — but to be killed so, without ceremony, without purification, in a field at night, was beyond their comprehension.

Only Thyloss had heard the Queen's words, and only Thyloss could guess at the explanation.

'Pointless!' he muttered angrily to himself. 'Cruel and pointless!'

With his hatred grew fear. What was she yet capable of, this demon queen?

Ayan was beside him and touched his arm.

'Look,' he said quietly. 'It is not only the birds who have been at our friend.'

Thyloss looked where he pointed and could see that a great deal of the meat had been cut skilfully away.

He thought of the banquet. He would not be surprised if the guests were at this moment eating the flesh of a beast who had been given as a gift to bribe and placate the Queen's dark god, the Destroyer. Involuntarily, a chill went through him. Would this mean that the funeral guests were to be part of the gift?

A sacrificed animal was not usually eaten unless sanctified with elaborate and profound ritual.

The people around him were afraid. He could see it in their faces, hear it in their muted voices. What would his father do?

Dispel fear. Bring back good sense.

'Fetch wood,' he cried, 'and build a pyre. We will give Grey Wind an honourable end, and the prayers we say will undo much of the harm that has been done.'

There was hardly time for this before they were due at the Field of Challenge, but Thyloss did not care. He had now lost all respect for the Queen, and would stop at nothing to thwart her plans.

Relieved to have someone tell them what to do, the people rushed about and built a pyre. When it was ready Thyloss had them build a small platform beside it. They did not know what this was for, but they did as he commanded.

When it was done and the flaming torches were ready to set it alight, Thyloss leapt up on to the small platform and raised his arms above his head. The crowd, now considerably larger than when they had begun, fell silent and all eyes were upon him.

He lifted his eyes to the holy mountain and stood in such tense and listening quiet that no one stirred. All eyes were on him. They expected him to pray aloud — but he said nothing.

Even the scavenging birds in the trees were strangely silent. The whole earth seemed to be poised, listening. Gradually a great peace seemed to come into their hearts. They were in tune with something that was good. Something that did not punish and wantonly destroy.

One girl told her mother afterwards that she had been overwhelmed by the beauty that was in everything . . . the mountains, the trees, the sky . . . even the tiny grasses and the aromatic herbs . . . She resolved never to do anything cruel or ugly that would spoil the harmony of it all. Her mother kissed her and held her close. She had felt it too.

Suddenly Thyloss gave the sign for flame to be put to kindling and the first sound to break the silence was the crackle as the dry twigs were consumed. Swiftly the flame passed from twig to twig, swiftly the fire grew.

The crowd gasped as they saw Thyloss crouch to spring, and before they could shout to stop him, he was in the air.

Like an acrobat on a living bull, he briefly touched the shoulders of the dead animal as he somersaulted over it. The flames reached up to him, but so swiftly did he move they could not take hold to burn him. He touched gracefully down upon the earth on the other side of the pyre, unharmed.

The crowd roared and Thyloss turned, his face shining with satisfaction.

'It is done,' he shouted. 'The Dark Lord will not have this bull. His soul is for healing by the Lady of the Lilies!'

The crowd roared again with approval, some because they knew of the Lady and held her in secret respect, others because it sounded good, and they were carried away by the excitement of the occasion.

'Now!' cried Thyloss. 'To the Field of Challenge, and the funeral games!'

Ayan watched him as he strode off, the crowd following him unquestioningly. His old eyes shone with happy tears as he thought of Quilla and Miron and how proud they would be of him.

8

The Dance

The dance Queen Nya-an had chosen for the funeral of her son was a spiral dance associated since ancient times with the goddess of the sacred groves and mountains. The slow coiling and uncoiling of the line of dancers to the centre and out again was reminiscent of the type of maze used by the votaries of the Goddess.

That this dance should be done now as part of the Bull Cult was unusual enough, but the Queen had changed the music, so that although the same thread of rhythm was there, it had a dark and sombre sound. The joy that was so much a part of the old dance was gone.

The guests, already uneasy after Ierii's outburst, were further depressed by the tone of the music.

Round and round went the dancers, linked together by their arms upon each others shoulders, coiling slowly and inexorably to the centre of the great court, where a priestess of the Bull Cult stood beside a small altar adorned with horns. There were many there who felt the spiral dance was a sacrilege at that time and in that place, but no one said a word.

At the centre the dancers bent their knees and pivoted low on the ground to turn. Over their heads the priestess chanted words that made it clear she was dedicating the dancers to serve the dead prince in the new role his mother had chosen for him, as a god who wielded power over the earth.

The Queen waved her hand and indicated that the guests should join the dance and, before they fully realized what was happening, they were gently, but firmly, directed by the Queen's attendants towards the dancers.

The bereaved mother watched from her throne on the west stairs with brooding satisfaction.

'You must join them too, my child,' she said to Princess Meri-an, when the last guest had joined the spiral.

The princess did not move. Her face was pale and set.

'Did you hear me?' the Queen said, a note of irritation in her voice.

The girl nodded, but still did not move. Her expression was terrified, but determined.

'Go. Join the dance. I command it!'

'No,' murmured the princess in a low, broken voice.

'What? What did you say?'

'I will not give myself into the power of my brother,' the child said more distinctly.

The Queen's eyes blazed.

King Ma-ii-nal, who was sitting as usual slightly behind his wife, hoping that she would not remember him and make him dance as well, forsook caution and leaned forward to defend his daughter.

'Perhaps it is not fitting for the future queen to do obeisance,' he said, clearing his throat.

Queen Nya-an rose and her expression was so formidable that the child could withstand her no more. Biting her lips and with lowered head, she joined the line of dancers.

'When I am queen,' she thought bitterly, 'things will be done differently.'

The king watched with aching heart as she sidestepped and stepped again, falteringly catching the rhythm of the others. He thought she had very little experience of dancing and did not expect her to be able to perform very well, but within a short while he realized, as did the whole court, that she was a natural dancer and moved lightly and gracefully. The music seemed to be inside her, her body expressing it outwardly.

Without realizing they were doing it, the musicians found

themselves subtly altering the pace, so that gradually they were playing faster and faster, fitting their music to the rhythm of the dancing princess. Everyone seemed to be aware of her and to follow her lead.

The whole character and focus of the dance changed. No longer were the horned altar, the priestess, and the words of dedication to the dead prince its centre.

The spiralling line broke up; the people formed a circle around the princess, clapping to the beat of the music. Faces that had been tense and anxious broke into smiles. Faster and faster she danced, pivoting to the music, sustained by the love in the hearts of the people around her.

Furious, the Queen found it impossible to break through the circle of attention centred on her daughter.

The girl's face glowed, her eyes shone. She had danced secretly before, in her chambers, where no one could see her. Now she was wild and free . . . nothing could touch her! She was no longer the pale shadow child of the palace . . . she was nymph of the sacred grove . . . priestess of the Lilies . . . her beauty was luminescent . . . her charisma potent.

As the music ended everyone in the hall, except the Queen and her attendants, cheered and clapped.

The noise was tremendous, and Ierii hearing it from her home, stopped weeping to listen.

'Enough!' the Queen cried, and this time, the cheering played out, her voice was heard.

She was standing, her arms raised, the gold snakes on her arms glinting in the sunlight that shone down on her from the sky above the open courtyard.

'The dancing is over. It is time for the challenge of Death!'

The spell of the dance was broken. The musicians and dancers left hastily through the north door, the guests, nervous about their role in the princess's defiance of the Queen, hurried to find their places in the procession that would follow the bier of the dead prince to the Field of Challenge.

The princess, suddenly feeling very small and deserted, walked back to her place, each step taking her away from her triumph and nearer to her mother's anger.

There were two high spots of colour on the Queen's otherwise pale face. She did not look at her daughter as she approached. Her eyes were smoulderingly fixed on something no one else could see, her lips grim. The king put out his hand to the princess and gave her arm a comforting squeeze as she joined him, fleetingly their eyes met and a look of great love passed between them.

In the interest of speed Miron had decided to leave the white bull behind. He left him with his drovers to follow at a more reasonable pace. Although he was no longer a young man, he could outpace many a youth. Stockier than his slender son Thyloss, he still had no surplus flesh upon him. All was muscle, bone, and energy.

Swiftly he covered the rocky ground, cutting through the mountains at a higher level than he would have been able to encumbered by the bull.

The image of Quilla teased his mind. She was seventeen summers older than when he had seen her last, but age had barely touched her. Her hair was white-silver, but her body was still firm and slim. He wondered if this was illusion. She had, after all, been in spirit-form when he saw her.

He had much to think about. When he had been with Quilla so many years before he had listened to what she had told him about the Spirit Realms, about the infinite levels of Being, about the Lords of the Sun who tried to open more of these levels to man on earth than they realized they had . . . and he had liked what he had heard. But, for some reason, he could not accept it totally, and she had not rushed him.

When he had said, 'I am interested – tell me more. But do not be disappointed if I cannot believe as you believe,' she had spoken but briefly of her beliefs, sensing that to press too hard on the matter would be a way to lose him.

Gently and persistently she had helped him to perfect his skills as Bull Keeper, knowing that in doing that he would be gradually training his body and his mind, sharpening his perceptions, until he was ready to make the leap in understanding.

Since she had left him Miron had experienced a great many of life's vagaries. He had known despair, rage, hopelessness. But he had also known determination and courage. He had learned to love his wife and his children in a protective, caring way – although the fire of his love for Quilla and Thyloss had never died.

There were times when he had longed to believe what Quilla believed, when he had looked at the magnificence of the sky and his heart had cried out, so loud that he felt it as pain, for there to be Someone, some Infinite and Omniscient Being, who could take the burden of decisions from him and tell him what to do.

But he could feel no Presence, and he turned away empty and lonely, neither following the rituals of his people's religion nor doing anything active against it. Accepting the one level in his life he was sure of, his role as Keeper of the Queen's Bulls, his role of father.

Now he found himself running over rocks, his heart pounding, on the strength of a vision he was already beginning to doubt that he had had.

He stopped short.

'What am I doing?' he thought. He had acted on impulse, not using his reason. This was unlike him. He sat down on a fallen chunk of limestone and buried his face in his hands.

'What *am* I doing?' he repeated, and listened to his heart beating fast and the roaring of blood in his ears. Quilla had always told him to be quiet when he was trying to think out something important.

'Go into the Silence,' she used to say.

He did not know how to do that, though he had watched her many times slipping into a strange deep quiet within herself where she did not even hear him if he spoke to her.

He tried to go over what had happened to him and explain it satisfactorily to himself.

It was understandable that he should dream of Quilla. He

had longed for her and dreamt of her many times. He must have been still asleep when he had 'thought' he saw her. Uneasiness about how Thyloss was managing could have caused him to imagine that Quilla was trying to warn him. It was his own anxiety that drove him over the hills so fast that he left his precious captive bull to follow with the drovers. He cursed himself for being such a fool, lifted his head, and determined to return at once to his men.

As he opened his eyes and stood up he was startled to find that everything around him had . . . changed.

He stared, bewildered, not believing what he saw, but unable to deny that he saw it. The landscape of sloping hillside and broad riverbed that was half pebble, half slender thread of water, the distant opening to the north where the sea plain of Ma-ii was, was still there but it seemed faint and insubstantial, and superimposed upon it were other scenes . . .

He seemed to be looking through a series of veils, each one a separate world, consistent with its own reality, but unaware of the others.

No, not like veils . . . the separate worlds seemed to exist in the same space . . . moving through each other . . .

He saw them.

He felt them.

What had seemed empty air was full of Beings so transparent that he could see an endless number of them by looking through them. He seemed to be able to 'hear' their thoughts . . .

He put his hands to his ears to shut out the sound . . . but he could in some way still 'feel' it!

Through this strange and luminous vision he could see Quilla, quietly pacing amongst trees and white stones . . . in and out she wove . . . the Beings flowing through her, and she through them.

He felt her quiet concentration. He noticed that where she was the movement of the Beings seemed to form a pattern, almost as though the energy she had was bending the space around her in some way, so that they began to be caught like twigs in a whirlpool and to flow spiralling to her centre, adding to her strength all the time, becoming part of her, giving their own energies to her . . .

He was overwhelmed with love for her and reached out . . . feeling the pull . . .

But even as he did so the element in him that had always withstood belief asserted itself, and he shook his head violently, dismissing the whole vision as some kind of aberration caused by his running too fast in the heat of the day.

He shut his eyes tightly, and then opened them.

The landscape was as he expected it to be, empty of anyone save himself. Sunshine on hard rock and clear air.

He was ashamed that he had even for a moment thought the vision had an objective reality.

But whatever he felt, and however hard he tried to convince himself that he had imagined it all, he did not in fact return to his drovers and the white bull, but continued on his way to Ma-ii as fast as quickly as he could.

9

The Challenge of Death

Bearers, wearing garlands of flowers and coronets of peacock and ostrich feathers, carried the corpse of the prince
encased in gold to the Field of Challenge.

Immediately behind them walked the Queen, her head
held high. Her dark eyes were dry, but lined so heavily with
black kohl that no one could see her expression. She was
followed by the other priestesses of the Bull Cult.

These women had been set aside from the community
from an early age and were looked upon with a great deal of
fear. Their training within the cult rooms of the labyrinthine
palace was secret, and they emerged as priestesses to the
public view only when they were ready, literally, to taste the
blood of the Bull sacrifice.

Their faces were heavily painted in a way that made it
impossible for anyone to recognize who they had been before they entered the service of the cult.

Their dress when they were attending a ceremony was
magnificent. Flounce upon flounce of rich cloth was in the
skirts. The short-sleeved bodices of woven gold thread were
cut back to leave the breasts exposed. The nipples were
painted gold. Bracelets of gold snakes with jewelled eyes
adorned their arms, and necklaces of carnelian and jet shone
at their throats. But their eyes . . . their eyes were glazed as
though they were under the influence of something, or someone, not seen by others.

In the procession behind them, musicians danced through
the narrow streets, playing gay and rousing music. In this

culture no funeral became gloomy until after the challenge and only then if the acrobat, the champion of Life, was killed.

The king and the princess walked together, their hearts heavy.

Behind them came the invited guests, followed by the bearers of wine and oil, fruit for refreshment, cushions for the court ladies to sit upon.

As the procession wound through the town, more and more people joined it to watch the games. Not many of them were concerned about the meaning of the ceremony, the private ambitions of the Queen, and the fears of the court. They were coming to see the acrobats, to cheer their favourites and to jeer at their rivals.

The Black Thunderer was a formidable bull and the excitement was high. The news had spread fast that Thyloss, the son of Miron, was to challenge the Thunderer for the prince. He was to dance with Death and if he came away unharmed after the ritual acrobatics had been performed over the bull's back, he would be cheered as the victor and it would be believed that Life had triumphed over Death.

Thyloss was greatly favoured by the crowds, being young and very handsome, much loved by everyone for his open and cheerful nature. Some of the acrobats kept to themselves and expected respect and honour wherever they went, sulking if they did not receive it. But Thyloss was one of the people, as happy as anyone to sit and talk over a jar of wine or play a game of tannat.

The noisy rabble bringing up the rear of the procession was chanting, 'Thy-*loss*!' Thy-*loss*!' as they walked, quite unconcerned that it was Prince Kel-urr they were supposed to be honouring.

Meanwhile from the south pasture another procession was approaching the Field of Challenge, but its mood was very different.

Thyloss was at its head and his face was angry. Behind him marched those who had seen the mutilation of Grey Wind and were anxious to see him avenged.

The Field of Challenge was an impressive place. When it had originally been laid out it was at the edge of the town, well beyond the streets and houses. But Ma-ii had grown considerably over the years and now, on all sides, it surrounded the vast arena.

On any day of challenge the flat roofs of the houses nearest the field were filled with people. On this day they seemed to be in danger of collapsing under the weight of the crowd. Every window was filled to capacity, every vantage point exploited to the full.

Behind the barriers that bordered the field and protected the spectators from being trampled or gored by the bulls, the crowds from Ma-ii, and those who had joined them for the day from the surrounding countryside and the other towns of the Island, waited expectantly for the events of the afternoon, excitedly chattering to pass the time. Jars of wine were passed among friends and many a reckless wager was laid on the outcome of the challenge.

At the west end of the field, forward from the barrier, but raised slightly on higher ground for protection, stood an elaborate wooden shrine to the fierce god of the Bull Cult. Along the front edge of the roof there was a formalized pattern of twenty-one pairs of bull's horns, and at ground level on a square wooden plinth in the centre was a huge golden double axe. The wooden pillars supporting the roof, characteristically thicker at the top than at the bottom, were painted deep red and black. The representations of the horns on the roof were gold, now gleaming brightly in the sun. It had not escaped the designer's notice that as the afternoon progressed and the sun sank lower and lower behind the shrine, the horns would cast dramatically long shadows across the field, taking their part in the final moments of the challenge.

When the royal procession arrived at the field for Prince Kel-urr's challenge of Death, it moved slowly and majestically from the great eastern gate to the shrine.

The still, gold-encased body of the prince was taken from

its bier and propped up against a small pillar to the left of the plinth of the double axe. It almost seemed as though he were still alive and standing to watch the outcome of the challenge. It was believed that the twenty-one pairs of golden horns above him, three times the magic number seven, would draw down from the mysterious regions beyond the sky the power of the great Lord of Death. As it entered the body of the deceased prince, it would strengthen it sufficiently to make it a worthy adversary at the moment of challenge.

Queen Nya-an took her place on the narrow, high-backed throne immediately to the right of the plinth, on a level with the prince, while King Ma-ii-nal and Princess Meri-an were seated farther back on lower, less ornate thrones, almost in the shadows.

The rest of the royal party were dispersed on either side of the shrine, those of highest rank on wooden chairs, those of lower rank on cushions spread upon the ground. But they were all raised slightly above the field by the rising ground on which the shrine stood.

The general populace crowded around the other three sides of the field, behind the light wooden barriers, restless and noisy. Enterprising entrepreneurs passed among them with food and souvenirs to sell, some even profaning the sacred Field of Challenge by climbing over the barriers and walking along the inside, the better to advertise their wares. Their calls mingled with the general hubbub, and the musicians playing beside the shrine had difficulty in making themselves heard.

When it was time for the games to begin, a huge thickset man gave the signal with the blowing of a large and powerful horn. The muscles in his throat swelled as he blew, the muscles in his almost naked body rippled as he flexed them: it was the moment he knew he had the attention of the crowd and he made the most of it.

The pedlars clambered hastily back over the barriers. The chattering ceased.

As the last notes of the horn died down the people cheered.

The gates to the field were flung back and two lines of acrobats ran into the arena.

Thyloss was not among them, but this did not perturb the crowd. They knew that it was customary to keep back the star performer until the moment of the Death challenge, which was expected to be the climax of the afternoon.

Some had heard the rumour about the sacrifice and were speculating about it, but most were content to enjoy the traditional games.

The acrobats ran and whirled lightly and somersaulted on the red earth. Naked youths and young girls with slim and beautiful bodies vied with each other to produce the most difficult and spectacular leaps and tumbles, twists and turns. Fast-moving music accompanied them and the cheers of the crowds encouraged them.

Even those of the court who had been disturbed by the events that had preceded this moment relaxed under the spell of the skill, grace, and vitality of the youngsters.

Dorran and Ierii had not dared to join the court party, although their rightful place was with them. They had followed behind with the crowds and had pushed their way, with the help of some who recognized and respected them, to a place on the eastern side, near the barrier and near the gate. They could see the whole field, the horned shrine, and the royal party, but they suffered from the push and shove of the good-humoured but restless people behind them.

At the finish of the preliminary exercise, another horn was sounded and the acrobats assembled before the shrine, fists to foreheads in respectful salute to the dead prince and the living queen.

The crowd grew expectantly silent and all eyes turned to the gate.

A piebald bull was led in and released.

It trotted quickly to the centre of the field, and paused for a moment looking around in surprise, not quite sure what was in store for it.

Certain of the acrobats remained before the shrine, where

they formed a kind of living safety barrier between the royal party and the activities on the field. Six others with perfect professional confidence approached the animal, taking up positions around him.

The crowd was silent, everyone held his or her breath, anticipation making each heart beat faster.

The sun beat down on the red dust of the field, on the gold covering of the dead prince, and on the beautiful poised bodies of the acrobats.

Suddenly three of them moved, teasing the bull, danced and leapt and spun around him so that he became frightened and confused, feeling threatened though they did not touch him.

Almost too swiftly for the audience to follow the detail of their movements, they worked around him until anger, the frequent successor of fear, took him over and he charged.

Then they were gone across the field and up onto the barriers; the three who had remained standing still, tensely watching his every move, swung into action now, dancing out of his way, doubling back to his rear, each in turn leaping and somersaulting over his back.

The crowd roared. The crowd shouted encouragement. The crowd cheered success.

The performance was good and the youngsters risked their lives at every move, but everyone knew that the bull was not as dangerous at the Black Thunderer, nor the acrobats as inspired as Thyloss.

When the bewildered bull was finally caught by drovers with nets, and led off exhausted, the cry was for Thyloss even before the cheers of appreciation for the others had died down.

But the time for Thyloss to perform had not yet come; there was no sign of him although Ierii strained to look along the fenced road to the bull pens to see if he was anywhere in sight.

Her heart was not in the games this afternoon. She longed only for Thyloss, thought only of the experience with Quilla and the strange, ominous feeling that the whole funeral ceremony was engendering. What did it all mean?

Fear was in her heart and she clutched her father's hand tightly.

After the piebald bull and the acrobats, there was a ritual sequence in which the dead prince was carried around the field for his people to pay their respects to him for the last time in his present incarnation. The priestesses of the Bull Cult performed a slow and dignified dance around his bier.

As they passed Ierii she hid behind her father, determined not to make the salute of worship to him. She had disliked him when he was alive and she loathed what he had come to stand for in death.

Her father stood straighter than he had ever stood; and as the prince passed, his face was set hard and he did not raise his arm. He met the eye of one of the priestesses and her dark eyes flashed over him as though storing up every detail of the scene in her memory.

The way of execution on the Island was by snake. It was not often used, but often enough to deter treason. In Dorran's own memory three people had been done to death in the pillar crypt of the palace by the deadly priestesses and their snakes. He had not known their crimes, but he had seen their bodies before burial, and the thought of them made him shudder.

But he still did not lift his arm to the Queen's new god as he passed.

After the prince had been returned to the shrine, the field was cleared for the climax of the afternoon. Again a hush came over the crowds as the last notes of the horn died down. All eyes turned to the gate.

Ierii emerged from behind her father, biting her knuckles with impatience to see Thyloss, and anxiety about what would ensue. She always watched him when he performed, but every time she swore to herself that she never would again.

'It is madness!' she told herself. 'One day he will be killed and I will be standing behind a barrier watching him when it happens.'

It was not uncommon for acrobats to be killed by a bull. When this happened the bereaved mourned even more deeply for the deceased, for it meant that the Lord of Death had won, and their beloved had no chance of rebirth on this earth.

If only Thyloss were not the champion today, Ierii thought. I would wish the acrobat to be killed so that Kel-urr would never return. She was startled at the fierceness of her own thought. Darkness had entered her heart and if she were not careful it would make its home there, but she was suddenly distracted by a cry from the crowd nearest to the bullpens. Thyloss had been seen striding along the path that was fenced off from the crowds, towards the main gate of the Field of Challenge. He was at the head of his team of acrobats and his head was held high, his eyes still blazing with anger at the wanton sacrifice of the bull, Grey Wind. The crowd went wild, shouting and cheering, throwing flowers. His kilt was red and gold, the band of gold binding his long hair back, gleaming in the sunlight.

'Thy-loss!' shouted the crowd. 'Thy-loss!'

Some people on neighbouring rooftops nearly fell off in their enthusiasm for their hero, but he took no notice of them and stared straight ahead. He was almost unaware of the noise around him, the petals that touched his cheek. He was thinking of Quilla's warning and the Queen's dangerous meddling with the ancient rituals.

When the team of bull leapers reached the gate of the Field of Challenge, the gate keeper moved forward to open it, but Thyloss stopped him with a gesture. He then looked back at the young men and women of his team.

'Are you ready?' he asked tersely.

'Ready,' they replied.

He took a deep breath and stood for a moment as though he were gathering his forces together. Then he ran lightly forward and vaulted over the closed gate, followed closely by the others, each uttering a wild high cry as they flew through the air. Once on the field their feet seemed barely to touch the ground they moved so swiftly over it, somersaulting and leaping in a dazzling display of acrobatics, covering as much of the area as they could so that all the crowd and not only the royal party could enjoy their skill.

If the other acrobats had been good, these were far better. The crowd was ecstatic and cheered and cheered again so many times the preliminaries were extended beyond their usual length.

Ierii, watching Thyloss, prayed for the black bull to be brought so that the whole thing could be over. Surely he was tiring himself with those leaps and somersaults? Was he showing off to the princess? Ierii stopped short with that jealous thought, and tears of shame came to her eyes. What a time to be thinking of such things! This could be the last bull dance Thyloss would ever dance. And indeed they themselves could all be dead in a short while if Quilla were right. She felt so restless and miserable she could hardly bear it. Where was the serenity so many people had commented on, where the strength she had learned from being quiet on the rocky hill behind her house? Where was the wisdom Quilla had tried to teach her? Her father saw her distraught face and put his arm about her shoulders. She blinked the tears back.

Thyloss executed a brilliant double backward somersault in the air and came to land before the Queen. He was too far from Ierii for her to see his expression, but if she had she would have been astonished at its challenging ferocity.

The Queen, face to face with his anger, was startled and shivered momentarily as a thrill of fear ran through her. But the ceremony had progressed too far for her to abandon it now; and she was determined to see it through.

She lifted her arm to signal that the horn should be blown. The note sounded and the black bull was released onto the field.

Thyloss turned to join his team and forgot the Queen in the danger of the moment.

The crowd was amazingly quiet, watching the Black

Thunderer's muscles rippling as he charged around the field.

At first the bull did not notice the little knot of acrobats waiting for him, but snorted and sniffed the air, glad at least to be out of his pen. He was almost unaware that all eyes were on him, sizing him up.

No one noticed the Queen leave her seat and step forward onto the Field.

The Thunderer slowed down. He had noticed Thyloss and his group. He stopped short not far from them, watching them as warily as they were watching him.

The crowd was silent. Everyone was concentrating on the bull; wondering what would happen. Slowly, cautiously, the acrobats moved into position for the Challenge, and then a gasp went up from the crowd. The Queen was seen walking across the field towards the bull. Thyloss only realized this when the Black Thunderer turned from him and directed his attention to her.

Thyloss moved at once towards her, slowly, warily, so as not to startle the bull into a charge.

'How now, my lady,' he said when he reached her, and there was a harsh edge to his voice, 'are you here to take my place?'

She did not seem to hear, but walked straight ahead as though she were in a trance, staring at the bull. It was as though she were locked in some experience not visible to the eyes of others. She and the bull stared at each other, each now seeming to be half animal, half human.

There was no sound from the crowd that waited, no sound from Ierii, who stood, tense with fear, biting her knuckles yet again; and no sound from the princess and the king, who had risen from their thrones.

No sound. Even the air seemed taut and stretched.

Suddenly the air seemed to vibrate and the rumbling of distant rocks falling reached their ears. The earth beneath them began to shake, and the beast, in terror, charged. The crowds screamed.

Quick as light, Thyloss leapt and turned the fatal horns

away. Unharmed, the Queen lifted her arms as priestess and cried in a voice louder than the thunderous growl of the earth . . .

'My lord! I am your queen. Take me!'

The black bull turned and again Thyloss leapt to divert his charge. Again and again the beast seemed to be trying to kill the Queen and again and again he shook Thyloss off like a troublesome horsefly.

The other acrobats had fled; chaos was everywhere . . . people were falling down with the shaking of the earth and those that were still on their feet were trying to get away. The walls of houses were cracking and stones and gourds that had been placed on roofs were tumbling into the streets.

'Mother of the Earth!' sobbed Ierii. 'Save Thyloss! Lady of the Lilies, help us!'

Her father was trying to protect her from the surging crowd and get her away in safety, but she would not leave without Thyloss.

Suddenly a scream louder than any other rent the air. Those near the shrine saw it topple and fall. The gold-painted casing in which the embalmers had placed the body of the prince split open as it fell to the ground. The corpse fell out. The mask of gold was knocked off, and those nearest looked directly into the ghastly grinning face of the dead youth.

The princess started to shriek hysterically, incapable of moving from the spot. Her personal servant, the young boy Da-yi, seized her and carried her away. She did not see the rest of the shrine crashing to the ground and the king, her father, falling with it.

On the Field of Challenge the Thunderer charged again, and again the Queen stood her ground before him and only Thyloss saved her life.

At first in her private ecstasy she seemed unaware that the earth was shaking. Perhaps she thought it was the bull that caused the ground to tremble. But then suddenly something in her face seemed to change, and she turned and ran towards the shrine.

'It is not complete!' she was crying. 'It is not complete! You must not leave!' she screamed to the crowd. 'I forbid you to leave!'

For a moment she looked with horror on her son's face and then pulled the golden ritual double axe from its place on the plinth.

Thyloss, still trying to control the bull and get others to help him, for the ground had stopped shaking, was startled to see the Queen return, whirling the golden double axe above her head until it blazed like fire.

'No!' he shouted. 'No!'

But his voice was choked as the bull's horn caught him in the side and he was sent spinning and skidding into the dust.

Looking up through sweat and whirling red clouds of dust, he saw the double axe flung so high above the Queen's head it seemed to split the sun in half, and, as he fell into darkness with the pain, it seemed to him that the sun had been killed and that their bright universe was finished.

Ierii reached him as his body went limp, and dragged him from the field in her arms.

Neither saw the fiery blade cleave the black bull's head, the blood spurt from the wound . . . the priestesses rush forward with crystal vessels to catch the precious liquid . . .

10

The Return of Miron

Quilla had not been at the Field of Challenge that afternoon, nor witnessed the strange and violent events that had taken place there.

Since dawn she had felt great unease and in the afternoon had gone to her maze in the sacred grove to calm herself. It was while in the centre of the maze holding the seven white crystals that she had had an overwhelming conviction that Ierii would bring Thyloss to her before nightfall on that very day. Her heart being troubled with a heavy premonition that the disaster she had foretold for Ma-ii was not far off, she could not 'see' as clearly as she would have liked the events that would lead up to the meeting with her son.

She returned to her cave and waited.

At the trembling of the earth, her own heart had trembled and she had wondered if this was the beginning of the end. But even as she thought this she chided herself. What end did not bring with it a beginning? What beginning, not an end?

At the edge of the Field of Challenge Dorran and Ayan found Ierii weeping over Thyloss. She was soaked in his blood and as pale as he was. Dorran tried to pull her from the lad, but she would not let him go.

'Is he dead?' Ayan asked softly, touching Dorran's arm.

Ierii heard him and denied it fiercely. Her father put his fingers on the young man's chest and shook his head.

'No, he is not dead, but the beat of his heart is very faint.'

'We must take him to a healer,' Ayan said urgently.

The two men looked at each other. Neither spoke of it, but both knew to whom they would take Thyloss.

'Come,' Dorran said gently, but firmly, to Ierii. 'We will take him to the Lady Quilla. She is the only one who can help him now.'

Ierii allowed herself to be eased gently away from him and watched as Dorran and Ayan lifted him between them. She followed as they left the town, her heart numb with anxiety and despair.

The earth was still now, as though it had never moved, and in the hearts of everyone, though there was unease, there was also the hope that the worst was past and Quilla's prophecy had already been fulfilled in the present disruption of the town. Here and there fires had started and it was because of the confusion caused by these that no one saw them leave. Afterwards, when order was restored, and no trace of Thyloss and the others were found, it was thought that they had perished in the fire.

By the time Dorran, Ayan, Thyloss and Ierii reached Quilla's cave in the mountain she had already seen them approaching and was preparing a potion of herbs and healing powders for her wounded son.

Out of breath, the two old men laid him on the rugs Quilla had made ready for him, and stood back respectfully as she leaned over him. No words were necessary, and no words were spoken.

Ierii stayed with him, cradled his head upon her lap, held him close while Quilla removed the rough makeshift bandage they had put on him, and bathed the ugly wound with herbal medicines. If Ierii had not been so concerned for Thyloss, she would have noticed the tenderness of the Seer's gaze as she looked at Thyloss. Seventeen years had passed since she had had to let him go, but in that time she had seen him several times, though herself unseen, and her pride in him and love were very deep indeed.

When Quilla had dressed the wound to her own satisfaction

and bound it first with healing leaves and then with clean cloth, she brought a bowl of fresh cool water and together she and Ierii washed away the dust and dirt from his face and limbs.

Dorran ventured at last to speak.

'My lady Quilla,' he said softly.

She looked at him over the bowed head of Ierii.

'My lord Dorran?'

'It is said you are now a great Seer.'

She smiled fleetingly.

'Many things are said.'

'I remember you well, my lady,' Ayan said respectfully. 'The greatest bull leaper we ever had!'

'And I remember you,' she said, looking fondly at him.

'It has been a long time . . .'

'A long time,' she repeated softly after him, looking at her son, still lying unconscious . . . regretting all the lost years.

And then the two men told her of the day's events. She listened quietly, filling in what they left out from her own understanding of the Queen and the people of Ma-ii. She looked sadly at Dorran.

'You and Ierii cannot return to Ma-ii. The Queen in her present mood will strike at all who have crossed her.'

'Ierii too?' Dorran asked. 'For myself exile is nothing. My home is wherever plants grow, and Ayan here has finished his work with bulls. But the children . . .' And he looked at Thyloss and Ierii.

'Their work is just beginning,' Quilla said sadly. 'It will not be easy.'

Ierii looked at her in alarm.

'What work, my lady? Can we not rest awhile?'

'There is no time to rest, Ierii. We must ride the wave as we find it!'

'But Thyloss is ill and in pain!'

'Is he?'

Quilla bent forward and looked at her son.

She laid her hands very gently over the place where he

had been gored. The cave was strangely quiet. Ierii saw a subtle change in Quilla's face, difficult to put into words, but very real. It was as though she had become receptive to something beyond her and was waiting patiently while it passed through her to the young man lying beneath her hands.

For the first time since the bull had gored him his eyelids flickered and he opened his eyes. He looked round in amazement at the quiet scene. Where were the crowds, the dust, the noise, and the violence? Around him loving, gentle faces were gathered. Behind them the dim recesses of the cave quietly waited. He turned his head and looked at the Lady Quilla. She was as beautiful as Ierii had claimed, but what Ierii had not been able to convey in words was the impression she gave of great age and yet of youth. She was like a spring of water in the mountains that had been there since the ancient days and yet was perpetually fresh and new.

She stooped and kissed his forehead, but said nothing. If he had had any doubts before that this was his mother, he had none now. It was as though he had always known her, as though something that he had only dimly been aware was missing in his life had been found and with it his life now had meaning. Of course Miron had loved her! He would not have been able to do otherwise.

Thyloss found tears welling to his eyes and turned his face from her. Ierii knelt beside him and tucked rugs closely around him.

'Thyloss,' she whispered, 'O Thyloss!' And this time her tears were of joy.

'He should sleep now,' Quilla said softly, 'come, we will leave them.'

She drew the two men quietly from the cave and left Ierii watching over Thyloss who was already breathing quietly and deeply.

Outside Dorran looked appealingly at Quilla, sensing some great sadness in her expression.

'What is it?' he asked. 'Is there no joy to come for those young people?'

Her eyes were full of pain.

'I see separation,' she said.

'Has there not been enough of that?' he asked.

She shook her head slowly.

'There is more,' she said, her shoulders drooping at the thought.

'Ierii and you cannot return to Ma-ii, but Thyloss and Ayan must go back. Thyloss is needed.'

'Thyloss is his own man. He might choose to stay with Ierii.'

'This is not the time for choice.'

'Every time is the time for choice!' Dorran said defiantly, growing angry with the thought of the suffering separation would bring to Ierii.

'Then Thyloss will choose to go!' She spoke with conviction. Dorran turned from her so that she would not see the tears in his eyes.

When Miron felt the second tremor stronger than the first, he was already at the pass above the plain of Ma-ii and could see the town in the distance. He could make out the crowds at the Field of Challenge to the east, but was too far away to see what was happening.

At one point, just as the tremor died away, he was nearly blinded by a sudden flash of light reflected off something on the field. Later he was to learn that it was the golden double axe spun by the Queen in her moment of frenzy.

Thyloss was in danger. Quilla had hinted at it and he now felt it with a terrible certainty, but the rocks the shaking earth had thrown in his path slowed him down.

When he at last reached the town he found the tremor had done some considerable damage. Houses were cracked and some streets impassable with debris, but more disturbing than this he found that no one wanted to talk to him. Several people he knew hurried down side streets when they saw him.

He made for his home as quickly as he could and there found his wife weeping. One quick glance around the room told him Thyloss was not there.

'Thyloss?' he demanded.

His wife lifted her tearstained face to his and her eyes were full of despair.

'Where is he?'

She shook her head, her heart so full she was unable to speak.

'Where?' he shouted, shaking her by the shoulders.

'Leave her alone,' one of his younger sons cried out. 'We do not know where Thyloss is. Everyone says he is dead!'

Miron spun around.

'Dead?'

The word dropped like a stone into the room. *Dead.*

'They say the Black Thunderer killed him when he tried to save the Queen,' the boy continued. 'Ierii tried to save his body and then they were both burnt in the fire near the Field of Challenge.' The child's voice broke.

But dead! Miron thought, and his mind could get no further than that word. He did not want Quilla's other realms and other lives. Was he to have no one he loved in *this* realm, in *this* life?

His daughter put her arm around her mother and he looked at them and realized that they were suffering as much as he. The death of Thyloss was a tragedy that would affect them all. His face softened and he took her in his arms.

'Tell me,' he said gently. 'When was this?'

He could not get the flash of light he had seen from the pass out of his mind. Was that the moment of his son's death? He had felt at the time there was something strange and significant about it. His face grew hard as he listened to the story of the past two days. His family knew only parts of it, but what they told him was enough to make him leave at once and make for the palace. His wife called after him, but he did not hear her as he strode through the darkening streets.

When he reached the palace he found his way barred by

guards. This was unusual. There had never been need of guards. The Queen had always been protected by the respect of her subjects.

'I am Miron!' he said angrily to the young men who barred his way with a spear. 'Let me pass!'

'No, my lord, it is forbidden,' an older guard said politely, but firmly.

'I am the Keeper of the Queen's Bulls! Let me pass!' he roared.

The two looked at each other as Miron put up his hand and advanced commandingly. The guards stepped aside, uncertain of their role. Miron was well known to them. He hurried past them through the passage that led from the south entrance into the great courtyard.

He had never seen the place in such disarray. Broken earthenware and spilled soil was everywhere. Dorran's precious plants lay wilting on the paving stones. Where were the servants?

The courtyard was deserted.

He strode through the palace to the Queen's chambers, meeting no opposition. When he did see attendants they seemed distraught and frightened and were hurrying from him.

On the stairs leading to the northwest wing, he found the crouching figure of Princess Meri-an. Her clothes were torn and her face scratched, blood and tears and dust mingled on her pale cheeks. She hid her face in her hands when she saw him and turned to the wall.

'My lady!' he said, stopping short. 'My lady princess . . . child . . . what is it? . . . What has happened here?'

She did not answer, but her distress was palpable.

His resolution hardened. The Queen was the key to it all. He must find her.

In the first audience chamber he found the bronze tripods that usually held the lamps overturned, furniture on its side, screens broken, but the personal rooms of the Queen beyond seemed to be untouched. The scene in her favourite day room took his breath away.

Everything was in order. Everything was apparently as it had always been. It was as though nothing had happened.

The Queen was seated on a couch with her back to him, gazing out to the distant sea. Her ladies were moving about the room doing what they always did, folding robes to be placed in the large chest beside the east wall, fanning her with feather fans from Africa.

At his entrance the picture seemed to freeze. The women looked at him and then at the Queen, a shadow of uncertainty crossing their faces. Slowly she turned and looked at him.

Stocky and fierce, he stood in the doorway, overpowering the room with his presence – the mountains he had come from – the journey he had just completed – the hard physical trials he had endured and the loss he had suffered, making a statement that could not be ignored, though he spoke no words.

Her face as she turned was beautiful and cold, a painted mask that belonged to no one. But as her eyes fell on him they sparked with sudden fire. She uttered a greeting and rose from her couch, her arms outstretched to his, her face filled with recognition and longing.

'You have come!' she murmured, and her voice was hoarse with the emotions she had been keeping under control and now could no longer hold back.

He did not respond, but looked at her harshly with the eyes of a hostile stranger.

'What is this, my lady?' he asked coldly.

'My love,' she said, 'we have been together since the beginning of time and yet these few summers of separation have seemed longer than all the aeons before. Now there will be no more separation. Now we will be king and queen together as we should have been from the first!'

Miron frowned. There was something in her voice that disturbed him more than in her words. He looked at her attendants. Their expressions were guarded, but in the eyes of one he saw pity for the Queen, and as he questioned her with his eyes, she shook her head almost imperceptibly.

'I am Miron, do you not recognize me, my queen?' he said now.

She smiled and took a step towards him.

'I have always recognized you, my love – but you have not always recognized me. I knew it would take a death to do it.'

Did she mean the death of her own son, or that of Thyloss?

Angrily he stared at her. When Quilla had disappeared and he had thought Nya-an responsible, he would have killed her if he had been sure enough that she had harmed her. Now, if he found the Queen were responsible for the death of Thyloss, he would not be able to stay his hand.

'Why do you look at me like that?' Nya-an was puzzled by his expression, but not alarmed. 'I offered him every-thing . . . honour, my daughter, my throne . . . because he was your son. He loved me! He gave his life for me . . .'

'What!' shouted Miron. 'What are you saying, demon of the dark?'

She drew herself up with dignity and almost he could have pitied her for the sadness that crossed her face.

'Do you not love me yet? Must I have no one?'

'We can never be lovers!' shouted Miron. 'Can you not understand that. I would die rather!'

'No, no . . .' she said, her voice so strange and vague he could almost not bring himself to hate her. It was as though her body was there but her mind was somewhere else. She walked about the room as though she were dancing a very slow ritual dance to music that only she could hear. 'Death will not free you,' she said softly. 'Death will bring you to my bed.'

He stared at her in horror, realizing now without doubt that she was crazed.

Gently her women moved to her and tried to return her to her couch.

'No!' she said with unexpected firmness, pushing them aside. 'Prepare the bridal robes. My daughter will not be married. But I shall.'

Miron stared a moment longer and then turned on his heel. As he strode into the passage the young serving boy Da-yi, who had evidently been waiting there for him urgently pulled at his arm and indicated that he must follow him, but be secretive about it.

So many thoughts were whirling about in his head that he was not in any state to make clear decisions. He went with the boy. The lad had a troubled, gentle face and a kind of inner strength that appealed to Miron. He reminded him somewhat of Thyloss, though he was younger and not so handsome. They left the Queen's quarters and went down the narrow connecting passage to the king's.

The wooden door that led to the king's private chamber had fallen to one side. The boy drew Miron inside and then stepped behind him so that he took the full impact of what lay in the room.

On the floor was the body of the king.

As though he were a sacrificial victim, he had been killed with the golden double axe, which now lay discarded beside him. Around him the wooden furniture of the room was splintered and broken. It was plain there had not even been the dignity of ritual in the sacrifice.

'The Queen?' he whispered to the boy, horrified, the room so silent he was loath to make a sound.

Da-yi pulled him urgently by the hand, but did not answer the question.

'We must go. They must not find us here!'

'They?'

The boy looked so fearfully over his shoulder that Miron asked no more questions but followed him at once. It was clear that it was not the Queen alone who had wreaked such havoc in the palace.

The boy led him back to the main stairs, looking around every corner carefully before he proceeded. When they reached the stairs Miron had so recently and so angrily climbed, the frail figure of the princess was still there.

'Help me!' the boy said to Miron, putting his arm around

the Princess Meri-an. 'We must take her away from the palace . . . away from Ma-ii!'

Miron knew that – this was not the time for questions. There would be time for those later. He had seen enough to know a great evil force was at work in the palace of Ma-ii, and the young child on the stairs must not be allowed to fall victim to it as had the kindly king and possibly his own son.

He would have lifted Meri-an in his own strong arms, but the boy Da-yi insisted on carrying her. She turned to him with a confidence she had not shown to Miron, and they hurried down the stairs back to the courtyard.

But leaving the dark palace was not to be as easy as entering had been. The courtyard was no longer empty.

Suddenly Miron knew who 'they' were, those that the boy feared.

Drawn up in ranks facing the stairs, as though waiting for his appearance, were the priestesses of the Bull Cult, formidable in all their ritual clothes, gold snakes upon their arms, live pythons coiling about their waists.

'Miron, hold!' the chief among them cried. Her hand with long gold-painted nails was raised against his progress.

Swiftly he turned his head but he could find no way out. Behind the women, the entrances were blocked by guards. This time they did not look as uncertain about their duties as the first ones he had encountered had been.

'Go back!' he whispered to the boy. 'Take the princess and try to find another way out. Make for the mountains. I will hold them for a while.'

Like a shadow Da-yi moved, Meri-an now on her own feet beside him, clinging to his hand.

Miron leapt down the stairs, shouting, hoping he could distract them from the youngsters.

He succeeded, and no one pursued them; they were concerned only with him. Halfway down the steps his flight was suddenly blocked. No one touched him. No wall was there. But as suddenly and as surely as though there was, he was brought to a halt, the wind knocked out of him. Again and again he tried to move forward. But an invisible barrier prevented him. The women, hard-eyed, stared at him, each with raised right hand, palm painted with strange devices.

Suddenly he was afraid.

He was a strong man and could fight wild beasts if necessary, but this was something he did not understand and did not know how to handle. He had never liked the priestesses. He had never worshipped at their horned shrines, but he had thought of them always as harmless.

'This is not happening!' he told himself fiercely. 'This cannot be happening!' But it was.

And then he noticed something he had not seen when he last passed through the courtyard. The plants that had been thrown out of their containers were not only wilting; they had been deliberately ripped and smashed. They had been stamped on and crushed as though their absolute destruction was of great importance. Threads of memory about the Cult of the Lady of the Lilies crossed his mind.

Had all plants become symbols of the rival cult to the Queen and her priestesses, and were all green growing things now to be destroyed as representing the hated religion that spoke of light and love and growth, instead of power and obedience and sacrifice? The thought made him angry, not so much in defence of the religion for its own sake as because it was Quilla's religion.

He tried to move forward again.

'Hold!' the chief priestess said again, and her voice went through his head like a shaft of pain. He stood still, accepting at last that he could not move.

'Why do you keep me here?' he demanded, not yet ready to surrender. 'I would go about my business.'

'Your business is with the Queen!'

'I have seen the Queen,' he said. 'I now go to find my son for burial.'

'There will be no burials,' the witch-woman said, 'until the prince has been given a new body.'

What did this mean? What did they intend?

114

He had heard of the prince's death and how the earth tremor had caused his gold casing to break apart and his body to spill out. He had not heard what had happened to him after that. His wife had not spoken of a burial.

'The king is dead. Is that your work?' he asked haughtily.

'He opposed our lady. He had to die,' she said simply, her eyes as cold as the snakes that coiled about her body.

'And if I oppose your lady, will I have to die?' he asked.

'You will not die,' she said flatly. 'You will lie with the Queen and cause the prince to be born again.'

'Never,' he shouted.

Finding himself free of the invisible barrier as the women dropped their hands as suddenly as they had raised them, he stepped forward.

They snapped their fingers, gold sparks shooting from their nails. As though this was a signal, a small, brightly patterned snake that had been slithering on the floor in front of the chief priestess darted forward with unimaginable speed and drove its fangs into his sandalled foot.

He felt the prick of it but took no notice; he thought only of crashing his way by brute force through the women, his temporary fear of them having disappeared when they lowered their hands. Surprisingly they drew aside to let him pass.

He believed they now feared him and would no longer impede his progress. But at the back of his mind a small anxiety began to grow. They did not look afraid. They were smiling, as though at a secret triumph.

He was almost at the door before he noticed the dull numbness that was creeping through his limbs, and the darkness that started at the periphery of his vision and closed in, circle by circle, till all light was extinguished and he fell like an axed tree with a thud on the hard stone paving at their feet.

11

Visions

Thyloss felt very drowsy after his strange healing and slept a long time in Quilla's cave. Ierii lay beside him listening to his breathing, occasionally propping herself up on her elbow so that she could gaze lovingly at his face, stroke his hair, or touch his brown cheek with her lips. Occasionally she dozed off herself, dreaming of being loved by Thyloss.

When he finally awoke he was completely refreshed and rose to greet the friends who were once again gathered round him.

Quilla gently removed the cloths and leaves from his wound and revealed that the wound had almost healed.

'It seems,' he said in a low, husky voice, 'you and I are not strangers to one another, lady, and I have more to thank you for than the healing of my wound.'

She smiled and took both his hands in hers. 'You have nothing to thank me for, Thyloss,' she said. 'The life you have was your own before I ever gave you entrance to this particular time and place, and as for the healing, that is thanks to the spirit force beyond us all.'

Thyloss began to move about the cave, stretching, flexing his muscles, testing his strength.

He came to a standstill once again before Quilla. Frowning he said: 'I feel restless. As though there is something I should be doing . . . but I do not know what it is.'

'Leave us and walk on the mountain Thyloss,' Quilla said. 'Allow yourself silence. Think.'

'Surely he is not well enough yet?' Ierii said quickly. 'He

should rest as much as possible!' She could feel the inevitable flow of time and change already taking him away from her.

Quilla put her hand upon her shoulder gently, soothingly. 'He is well enough,' she said. 'Come with me, child of a prayer, help me gather food for our meal. We must all eat before we face what is next required of us.'

Dorran and Ayan prepared the fire, while Quilla and Ierii went in search of herbs and leaves.

Thyloss sought guidance from the Spirit Realms.

The mountain peak was jagged and uneven, the white quartzite veins standing clear of the bedrock in many places like complex and beautiful sculptures.

Thyloss wedged himself against the wind between two upright slivers of crystal. Below him he could see Ma-ii, the plain and the sea.

What was it that he felt he must do?

He worried at the question, but no answer came to him. Only more questions.

After a time he forgot what it was that he was asking and why he had come to the mountaintop. He let the visual splendour of the place take his attention. His eyes followed the plants that grew out of the cracks and crevices in the rock, watched how the wind tugged at them and yet they held firm . . . admired their various patterns . . . their subtle harmonies of colour.

Beyond them he noticed the shapes of rock, the shades of earth . . . the trees . . . the roots that held to the earth that the leaves might benefit from heaven . . .

He could see the fields where he had trained for the Bull games, the gymnasium where he had learned to somersault and leap. Ma-ii itself seemed so small he was ashamed to think that he had once thought it of such great importance.

Even as he thought this, another 'thought' came to him that did not feel as though it were his own. He knew that he was at once a small point among an immensity of small points, and yet he (and indeed each one of those points) was the pivot on which the whole magnificence of the universe turned.

He felt suddenly very excited.

A film seemed to have been removed from his eyes and he saw, as it were, through the surface skin of the city on the plain . . . He saw a strange dark mist curling through the streets and around the houses, blinding the people . . .

He saw into the courtyard of the palace as though he were directly above it, and superimposed upon the pattern of paving stones he knew so well he saw another pattern . . . of strange and linked devices such as he had never seen before.

He stared harder, straining his eyes, and saw that patterns were formed by the figures of the priestesses as they stood about the courtyard. He could tell the pattern was planned. It was some secret rite, some invocation of the geometry of magic. He did not know then that the devices he saw were the same that Miron had seen painted on the palms of their hands.

He began to feel as though he were choking . . . a dark mist was closing in on him and he was no longer above, but lurching from street to street . . . seeking something . . . someone . . .

He knew the women must be stopped. As each moment passed he could feel the power they were invoking gathering strength. Then he heard a thundering sound, a roaring and a tearing.

He turned in terror in time to see a herd of bulls, with horns of gold and black, steam rising from their flanks, charging towards him.

He called and leapt as he had been trained to do . . . but this time his leap became flying and he was once more above the scene, staring down with horror as the beasts stampeded through the town, knocking down buildings, trampling all to death . . . making for the Field of Challenge, where rising like some giant and fiery cloud, a black bull of immense proportions rose on its hind legs – drawing the others to it . . .

Again Thyloss saw what his normal eyes would not have been able to see.

He saw the face of the black bull.

It was the face of the dead prince.

And then he saw a figure dragged through the broken town in chains . . . and when he looked closer, it was the figure of his father . . . the Queen leading him by the throat and hauling him before the black bull.

'Now!' she screamed, and raised her arms, the gold snakes flashing.

Daggers of light suddenly blinded him.

Ierii found Thyloss, slumped in a faint, still wedged between the crystal columns of the mountain peak.

'You see!' she cried. 'I knew you were not really well yet!'

Tears streamed from her eyes as she put her arms around him and held him close.

As the first light of the following day started to touch the mountains, Thyloss and Ayan slipped from the cave and made for Ma-ii.

Ierii was still sleeping and Thyloss paused as he passed her, leaning over her, scarcely seeing her in the dark cave but feeling her presence strongly and smelling the scent of flowers that always seemed part of her. If someone had told him a few days before that he would have felt so loath to part with her he would not have believed him.

He did not see Quilla in the corner, eyes wide open, watching him. Her prayer for his and Miron's safety went with him, and her heart ached to see him go.

Ierii wept long and bitterly when she woke and her father told her what had happened.

'I must go with him!' she said at once, preparing to leave.

'No!' Quilla said with unaccustomed sharpness. 'You will hinder him.'

Ierii looked at her, shocked. How could that be?

'I love him. I cannot live without him. If he dies, I die.'

'If he dies, you will not die. You are needed,' Quilla said firmly.

Ierii shook her head fiercely.

'I am nothing without Thyloss.'

'He needs you away from Ma-ii . . . and alive.'

Ierii looked as though she would protest further and then seemed to resolve to be silent. Her face was sullen as she joined in the morning prayers, and the words she prayed to the Lady of the Lilies never left her angry, fearful heart, and so could bring her no relief and comfort.

A few hours after dawn she slipped away and started to hurry down the mountain.

Dorran, when he first noticed that she was missing, told Quilla that he would go after her and bring her back, but Quilla shook her head.

'We must let her go. We must not hold her here against her will. If she returns it will be of her own choice, and will show that she is ready for the role she has to play. No one forced Thyloss to go. He chose.'

Dorran looked troubled, but understood that what she said was wise.

When Ierii had first climbed the mountain in search of Quilla she had come up the west side and so missed the sacred grove. In choosing now to follow a different route she came upon the place where Quilla had laid her maze and Thyloss had planted his lilies. She was so agitated it is possible she would have hurried by without noticing the significance of the place, had not her ankle turned on a stone and she was forced to sit down to rest it.

As the pain subsided she began to notice her surroundings. The morning sunlight flickering through the branches of the trees made brilliant patterns on the earth. Lilies suddenly catching the light on their wax-white petals seemed to glow as though they were spirit flowers and not of the earth.

The air was strangely quiet and still. The wind that usually soughed through the trees on this side of the mountain was absent and Ierii began to feel that she could almost touch the silence. The urgency she had felt but a short while before to follow Thyloss to Ma-ii, had dissolved like mist touched by the sunlight.

Out of the corner of her eye she thought she caught a movement. She turned quickly.

There was no one there, but the tree she gazed on was different from any she had ever seen. It crossed her mind that her father would be very interested to see it, and then she began to notice that every tree around her was different from every other tree, and most of them were kinds not common on the Island.

She began to realize that this was no ordinary wood she was in, but a sacred grove planted in honour of the Lady of the Lilies, the very grove Thyloss had visited. The pain in her ankle forgotten, she stood up and went from tree to tree, putting her hand against the bark, gazing up into the branches, silently asking for help.

The one she had first noticed gave off a strange and haunting scent when she touched it. She noticed some resin and rubbed it. The scent became stronger and invoked in her an inexplicable feeling of awe. Startled, she withdrew her hand and gazed up at the heavy, dark branches.

She thought about it for a while, and then, as though impelled, she built a tiny circle of stones, placing some of the resin on a little pile of dry leaves within it. She took two sticks and patiently rubbed them together. Her heart beat strangely as the thin thread of smoke rose to the sky from the fire she had kindled and the scent of incense filled the grove.

In the grass she noticed some white stones and as she followed them with her eyes she began to realize that they were laid out in the shape of a maze.

She took off her sandals and started to walk it. Slowly. Carefully. Step by step. She seemed to be walking a winding, invisible path into her own mind as the tall trees watched her and the smoke of the incense filled the air with its subtle and pungent aroma. At the periphery of her sight she sensed movement, but she kept her eyes on the white stones and her bare feet. She could have sworn the trees had moved and were crowding nearer her, but she knew this was impossible.

Reaching the centre, she suddenly looked up, wide-eyed and more alert than she had ever been. She was completely surrounded by Shining Beings.

The air above the incense vibrated and as she turned her attention to it, perhaps because she was directed to do so, though she could not be sure, she saw a faint and luminous landscape forming in the air. She stared in astonishment.

It was as though she had climbed the farthest ridges of the mountains that surrounded her home, and was gazing into a high and fertile plateau with mountains on every side of it . . . a kind of enclosed and secret place, cut off from the rest of the world.

'This is where you must go,' voices seemed to say.

'This is where you must take all who will come with you and you must start a new life. Plant trees, build houses . . . live as you were always meant to live . . . in love and harmony . . . the Bull and the Lily must be at peace – they are the two sides of the one reality – to worship the one without the other is to create imbalance . . .'

Ierii began to tremble. 'How can I do this?' she whispered.

'Go back to Quilla, child. Wait upon the mountain. Take those who come to you and teach them what you will learn in the Silence.'

'Thyloss?' Ierii suddenly cried. 'Will he come to me?'

But already the bright figures were fading – the incense was burning out.

'Stay!' cried Ierii desperately. 'Tell me more! Will Thyloss come?'

There was no answer. She was alone in the grove.

She looked around in despair and the grove that had seemed so transcendent and beautiful a moment before seemed very ordinary now. A cloud had crossed the sun. No bright light flickered through the leaves and already she could hear the moan of the wind as it creaked in the branches farther down the mountain. It would not be long before it reached her.

She wanted to rush out of the maze, crashing across the lines of stones, returning to Ma-ii and Thyloss as quickly as she could, in spite of what she had been told, but there was still enough magic in the grove to suggest to her that she should come out of the maze the way she had come in, slowly and deliberately.

When she at last stood beside her sandals at the entrance she was calmer and more controlled. She knew that experiences such as the one she had just had did not come easily and without reason. She had been honoured with a revelation and she respected the Beings of Light enough to know that they could see farther and deeper into the mysteries of life than she could.

Trust is a vital part of love, and she knew that she loved the Beings of Light and the Lady of the Lilies, and through them perhaps the Unimaginable, the Inexpressible, the Source of All.

Trustingly she turned about and began to climb the path that led back to Quilla's cave.

Dorran heard her approach and hurried to meet her. They kissed warmly, and climbed the rest of the way, arms about each other.

'What made you change your mind?' the old man asked.

Ierii looked into the eyes of Quilla, who was standing outside her cave, tall and slim.

'Do you know?' the girl asked her directly.

'Tell me,' the woman replied.

Ierii described what had happened as well as she could, but she found that the words made the experience seem more distant and more unreal. Somewhere, deep in her, it was still there as fresh and vivid as it had been . . . but the surface memory was already overlaid with doubt.

'What was the tree with the strange resin?' she asked, sure that that at least had been real.

They were sitting drinking fresh goat's milk from Quilla's small herd, in a place sheltered from the wind; the sun, released from its earlier cloud, blazed down on them. It would not be long before the warmth of late spring gave way to searing summer heat.

Dorran's plants would not survive long without his care.

'Frankincense,' Quilla said to Ierii dreamily, as though she were recalling a pleasant memory.

Dorran looked interested.

'I thought it was when you described it,' he said excitedly. 'It is the only one in this country.'

'Where does it come from?'

Quilla smiled.

'That is a long story.'

'Please tell it to me,' Ierii pleaded.

'Briefly then,' Quilla said. 'You have heard of the Queen Hatshepsut?'

'Of Egypt?'

'The same. Her mother's family came from our Island, and when Hatshepsut was a young queen she came to us for a pleasure visit with her chief adviser, Senmut.'

'Some said he was also her lover,' Dorran interjected. 'She brought with her that very tree to grow here in memory of her mother.'

'I well remember the procession to plant it," Dorran said.

'It was a very special tree,' Quilla said thoughtfully. 'Not only had it come all the way from Egypt, but before that it had been fetched with others from a country far to the south – Punt, I think it was called. The Queen Hatshepsut had been told in a vision by Amun, her god, to make his temple a garden and to look for these particular trees in that particular place. It amazed everyone that she sent such an expensive expedition so far and through such dangers – not for conquest or for treasure – but for trees!'

'Some people said such trees did not even exist!' Dorran said.

'Who was this Amun?' Ierii asked curiously. 'I have not heard of such a god.'

'Different people have different names for that which they seek. A different name does not necessarily mean a different god!'

Ierii was silent. How many names for the nameless one?

'I have been to Egypt in body and in spirit-form.' Quilla's eyes grew misty with memory. 'And I have seen the temple that she built. It is magnificent. It rises in three great terraces against a high stone cliff. On every terrace trees and flowers flourish. One could walk there in cool and shade in the heat of the day.'

'It is said that Amun himself has been seen there in the shade of the frankincense trees,' Dorran said. 'I met a Egyptian once who claimed he had seen the footprints of the god in the earth beneath them.'

'Strange kind of god to leave footprints!' Ierii laughed.

Quilla looked at her, amused.

'There are stranger things than that in the world, child.'

Ierii was silent, remembering her experience.

'Do you think the Lady Hatshepsut and her god had anything to do with what happened to me today?' she asked at last.

Quilla looked thoughtful.

'If she had . . . I wonder why.'

The beautiful queen was dead, her images defaced and her name forbidden in Egypt, the country she had ruled so long. Another pharaoh conquered men where she had conquered hearts. Exiled from her own home by death, did she perhaps seek expression in the land where she had once been happy, the land of her mother, and of her carefree days with her lover?

'The spirits that guide us are not always pure Spirits from

126

the Timeless Realms. Many are wanderers en route from one life to another. She might well be here, clinging to old memories.'

'If she is,' Ierii said, 'should I trust her?'

'In her last life she was extraordinary. It is said that at her coronation the temple dancers saw light shine through her, and when she joined them, barefoot and simply dressed before the ritual robing, splendour and magnificence surrounded her as though she were already in her finest robes and jewels.'

Quilla paused, and then continued as though thinking aloud.

'In some ways the power she had as pharaoh seduced her from the greater role she might have had as Seer. It was as though she were torn between two possible realms and she chose at last the lesser one. But in her youth she did see visions . . . and as a woman she did love deeply . . . Yes, Ierii, I think you may safely trust her.'

Ierii thought about the Shining Beings she had seen, but she could not be sure that one had been the Egyptian queen.

12

The Return of Thyloss

Thyloss and Ayan approached Ma-ii with caution, not sure what they would find there.

In the courtyard of his home they met one of Thyloss' young brothers. The boy stared at him in astonishment. Thyloss laughed and slapped him on the shoulder.

'Do you not recognize me? It is but a day since I have seen you – although I do admit it feels like many lifetimes!'

The boy looked at his shoulder where Thyloss' hand had rested in amazement.

'Are you spirit?' he whispered hoarsely.

'No, I am not spirit,' Thyloss laughed. 'Or, at least, not more than usual. What is troubling you?'

'We thought you were dead!' the boy cried. 'We were sure we saw the black bull kill you! And someone said Ierii had taken your body from the field and then . . . then there was the fire. Lots of people are still missing. Ierii and her father and . . .' Here he looked at Ayan with open mouth.

'And old Ayan too?' the old man said with a twinkle in his eye.

'Well, we could not find any of you, and there were those bodies no one could recognize . . .' He looked at Thyloss. 'We were wondering what to do because we could not find your body for burial.'

Thyloss and Ayan laughed.

'It is just as well, seeing that I was not dead,' Thyloss said. 'Come, let us go to the others.'

The lad led the way toward the kitchen area, still confused.

Thyloss was impatient to have news of his father and, as soon as the joy and wonderment at his miraculous recovery had subsided a little, he asked about him. The mood of the little family changed, and he knew by their faces that the news was not good. He had been wise to hurry back to them. He learned that Miron had returned the day before but that, on hearing of Thyloss' apparent death, he had gone to the palace.

'He was in a great rage, and he has not returned!'

Thyloss frowned.

'I will go and find him,' he said at once, turning to leave the room.

'No, wait!' Miron's wife cried. 'There are things you need to know. There have been great changes here.'

'What kind of changes?'

'The palace is guarded,' his brother said.

'The king and queen and princess have not been seen at all . . .'

'The prince's body disappeared from the Field of Challenge. But there has been no funeral. We do not know what this means.'

'Send Ayan first . . . no one will harm him.'

'Why should they harm me?'

'You are Miron's son.'

'But I saved the Queen's life.'

Miron's wife hesitated. She longed to have news of her husband, but did not want to lose Thyloss yet again. Although he was not her own son, she loved him and relied on him as though he were.

Friends and neighbours had gathered in the room while the family were talking, having heard rumours of the return of Thyloss and anxious to show their delight. Now they were full of advice, most of it impractical. Some wanted to march on the palace.

Thyloss would not hear of this.

'I will go,' he said. 'In peace. If I too fail to return, then will be the time to think of marching.' He knew that violence, once started, has a way of growing, destroying more of the innocent than the guilty, breeding problems greater than the ones it set out to solve.

There was murmuring, but all agreed to wait.

Thyloss set off for the palace; many followed out of curiosity, but kept well back, as he had requested.

When Miron opened his eyes he was in a dark chamber. He found himself lying on a couch surrounded by lamps on tall bronze tripods. He lay for what seemed a long while drowsily staring at the sputtering flames, only dimly aware that he was in fact awake and not in a dream. He felt lethargic and at first could not bring himself to move.

After a while he turned his head from side to side, tying to examine his surroundings. The flames of the lamps were so bright he could see little else. It was as though he was enclosed by walls of light behind which, in contrast, the darkness was unnaturally dark.

He raised himself on one elbow and looked down at his own body; he remembered how he had fallen, and wondered if he was injured in some way. As far as he could see he had suffered no harm. His body had been bathed and scented, and he stared in amazement at the fine pleated linen that had replaced his dusty working clothes. He sat up, suddenly alert, aware that things were not as they should be.

From the depths behind the lamps he knew he was being watched.

'You there!' he said boldly, angrily. 'Show yourselves!'

There was no answer, no movement. Fiercely he seized one of the lamps and pushed it aside, striding out from his square of light into the space beyond.

No longer blinded by the closeness of the lamps, his eyes grew accustomed to seeing, and he found that he was surrounded by the dim figures of the priestesses, erect and unmoving in the shadows, like statues. They made no effort to restrain him, but watched him with eyes that glittered ominously as he crossed the room and pushed his way through the curtained doorway.

He must have become disoriented by his recent experience, for he expected to be back in the corridor. Instead, he found himself in the Queen's bedchamber, a room beautiful with painted frescoes, with feathered African fans and delicately fashioned furniture.

The Queen herself was lying upon her bed, watching him.

He knew at once that he had been expected. He stopped short, turned, and looked for a way out that did not take him past the formidable priestesses. He had had a sample of their powers and did not want to have to confront them again.

The Queen smiled and moved her pale limbs.

'I have been waiting for you, my love,' she said. 'You have slept long.'

'I have not slept at all,' snapped Miron. 'Your witches put a spell on me! I do not know what has been happening here, but I am leaving now.'

There was no doorway except the one through which he had come.

So be it.

He turned to that. But his way was barred.

A priestess stood in the dark space, light falling on the marked palm of her hand as she held it up to him. He could not move towards her.

'There is no way out,' the Queen said silkily. 'Come, my love, why do you spurn me so?'

Desperately he looked around. She had left the bed and was walking gracefully towards him, the light wrap she wore falling away from her figure so that nothing was hidden.

She was indeed beautiful.

'You are beautiful, lady,' Miron said coldly. 'No one can deny that. But I will not lie with you!'

There was the slightest flicker of the old menace in her eyes, but it was gone in an instant and she was all warmth and gentleness again. She was close to him now and the scent she wore was making him feel strangely confused.

His vision began to blur again and he shook his head impatiently to clear it. She touched his arm and he pulled himself back from her, but the touch could still be felt.

Soft music was in the air . . . strings plucked by unseen hands . . . sweet and deadly scent . . . Gracefully she turned and turned again . . . touching him lightly with every turn . . . each touch more disturbing than the last . . .

He tried to hold to other things . . . to cling to old memories . . . but nothing seemed to exist outside the exquisite room and the beautiful woman . . . when her lips touched his at last and her limbs intertwined he resisted no longer . . .

He could not deny that he had pleasure, but the aftermath was bitter.

Angry with himself, he pulled away and opened his eyes.

He looked straight into the impassive gold face of the dead prince. With horror he realized the prince's body in the gold case had been beside the Queen's bed the whole time.

Did Miron imagine it, or was there a gleam of mockery in the sightless eyes of lapis lazuli?

'Mother of the Earth!' shouted Miron, leaping from the bed. 'What is happening here?'

The Queen laughed, and the sound was harsh and triumphant. How could he have found her desirable?

He stared at her now, and saw not a beautiful body but a casing of flesh on a dark and bitter soul. Around the room the priestesses were slowly pacing, softly chanting incantations.

He stood and gazed around the room, bewildered that he had allowed himself to be trapped into such a situation.

'Now you may go, my lord,' the Queen said mockingly. 'I have had from you all that I need. My son will live again!'

Sickened, he rushed from the room. This time no one tried to stop him.

Shaking with disgust and anger, he stormed through the palace, guards and servants all stepping out of his way and bowing low in mockery, as though they all knew what had happened.

When Thyloss reached the palace and demanded to see his

father, he was told politely that Miron had left the palace of his own accord early that morning, and that no one had seen him since.

At first Thyloss did not believe it and demanded to see the Queen. One of the servants was despatched to see if the lady would consider giving him audience. The reply was affirmative, and he was ushered into her presence. He had never seen her looking so happy.

'Thyloss!' she cried with genuine pleasure. 'I have much to thank you for, and I did not think you were alive to receive my gratitude.'

He bowed politely in greeting, but she could see the impatience in his eyes.

'You have come, I see, not to pay respects, but to make a demand of me,' she said, but even now there was no bitterness in her voice, only a slight wariness.

'My father, lady.' Thyloss said boldly. 'I want to see my father!'

'But, Thyloss, I do not keep your father from you. Is he not at home with his wife?' Her voice was too smooth for innocence.

'He was last seen yesterday entering the palace.'

She smiled, and there was something secret and gloating in her smile.

'I assure you, he is not here. You may search the palace if you like, but you will find no one hidden.'

Thyloss looked irresolute. She seemed to be behaving so reasonably, he could not believe she was holding his father prisoner. He looked around hoping to gain time to think what he should do next.

The palace had been cleaned and put in order since the day before, and Thyloss saw no trace of the disorder that had so disturbed Miron. But he could see that there was something different, something missing. After a moment or two he realized that there were no plants in the palace. All the hanging vines, the potted trees were gone and in their place strangers stood with spears.

'I am sure you will find your father, Thyloss. Look not so angrily at your queen. Smile at me. It is a good day. My son has found another body.'

Thyloss looked at her sharply.

He did not understand.

'Yes,' she said. 'He will live again on this earth plane, in this very palace. I have arranged it all.'

Thyloss looked his question.

'I know I spoke of him as god – but this will mean he can be with me in flesh and yet rule as god. You will see, this time he will be magnificent!'

Her eyes shone.

'Last time I chose the wrong father for him. This time there has been no mistake!'

Thyloss remembered what he had just recently learned about the Queen's interest in Miron.

Did she mean . . .?

The Queen clapped her hands and her attendants came gliding into the room.

'See, ladies, Thyloss has come back to us! It is truly a good day for us. Prepare a feast. We must welcome him and give him the honours of a hero.'

'I do not want . . .'

'No, do not protest, my beautiful young man. You saved my life. I will reward you. Do you want my daughter in marriage?'

She saw by his face that he did not.

'No matter,' she said lightly. 'I ordered you once to marry her – but that was when I was looking for a son. Now . . .' And here she placed her hands upon her womb and smiled triumphantly. 'Now I have no need of substitute sons. You need not marry the pale princess. Choose what you will. I will give you anything!'

Thyloss stood stunned. Anything? His head spun.

'But speak now – my generous mood may pass.'

He remembered the horrifying vision that had brought him back to Ma-ii.

'I want . . .' His voice caught in his throat and he almost lost courage to continue, but he knew what he had to say. 'I want the end of the exclusive power of the Lord of the Bulls, and the return of the Lady of the Lilies!'

Her face became distorted with dark rage.

'No!' she screamed. 'No!'

Suddenly the dread priestesses of the Bull Cult were around him as he had seen them in his vision. They circled him, their eyes like black fire.

He turned and ran, breaking out of the circle before the full power of their presence had closed it to him.

As he fled through the palace passages . . . it seemed to him he heard the thunder of hooves as he had on the mountaintop . . . He did not stop running until he reached his home.

'What is it?' Miron's wife cried, and his brother looked out of the door to see who was pursuing him. There was no one.

Miron did not return to his home when he left the Queen.

At first he was not aware of where he was going. He knew only that he wanted to get away – from the Queen, from the palace, and if possible from himself. He walked blindly through the narrow streets, by instinct making for the open country and the mountains to the south of the town.

He longed for Quilla in the way he had when she first left him. He could think of nothing else.

This time I will find her! His thoughts persisted on this one certainty. I *will* find her!

He could not feel the sharp rocks that tore at his bare feet, or the thorns that scratched at his legs. The sun burnt on his back with increasing intensity as he climbed.

He did not follow a path, and he did not plan his direction. Too long had he thought about Quilla and how to find her. Too long had he ignored her teaching about the nature of reality.

If she was right, they would find each other when it was

necessary for them to do so and no amount of effort on his part would affect the matter. He held her image in his mind as though it were a lamp and he were using it to find his way through the dark. Other than that, he thought of nothing.

Was this the 'going into the Silence' Quilla talked about?

Normally a busy man, Dorran could not sit still and let the day pass. He took Ierii with him to study the plants on the mountain, and to decide which ones would be most useful to cultivate if her vision of the plateau came to pass.

'These mountain plants will be more suited to the altitude of the plateau,' he said. 'Not many of the ones that grew so profusely in Ma-ii will grow easily there.'

'The place seemed a green and fertile one, Father. I saw waterfalls from the mountains, but strangely' – and here Ierii frowned a little, trying to recall a detail – 'strangely not many streams.'

'I expect the water went underground. These mountains are full of swallow holes and caves into which it could have disappeared. Do not be concerned. There will be ways of reaching it.'

'I am not worried about that,' Ierii said. 'But I am worried about finding the way there.'

'Those who told you to go . . . will show you the way.'

Ierii was silent.

Quilla was glad to have some time to herself. She, who usually had such great inner strength, was finding it difficult to be strong.

She tried to hold to all that she had learned of the different levels of Being and the interplay between them. She tried to call to the Shining Spirits . . . to the gentle but powerful Lady of the Lilies . . . She tried to muster her own strength that it might be beamed to those who needed it in Ma-ii . . . but . . . she could think of nothing but Miron and the love they had had between them . . . memories of lying with him in a field of flowers on a day in early spring and how they had laughed when their idyll had been ruined by the sting-ing of ants . . . memories of the way he looked at her, amused, when she was being too serious . . . memories of his touch . . . his kiss . . .

She rose suddenly from the boulder on which she had been sitting and walked about restlessly . . . trying to forget his kiss.

Why? she thought bitterly. Why today . . . why now . . . just when I need my control? Seventeen summers have passed and I can remember that as though it has just hap-pened!

Someone stood beside her, someone she could not see, shaking her head.

'Oh, Quilla! Quilla! Do not strain so! The harder you fight a thought, the more stubbornly it holds. Have you learned no tricks to outwit your mind in all these years? Or is it that you are meant to hold to Miron this day of all days . . .'

But Quilla did not hear the voice, and the pain of struggle did not leave her.

Quietly the spirit moved away.

Miron found Quilla. He came upon her suddenly.

She turned upon her heel and saw him standing on the mountainside staring at her. She caught her breath.

'How cruel some visions are!' she thought.

He too could scarcely believe that his searching was over. Neither dared move, afraid the other would disappear.

It was the screech of a bird close by that startled them and made them realize that the scene before them was ex-actly as they longed for it to be. Miron took a step towards her and so intense was the feeling between them that al-though they were still apart, they could feel the nearness of each other as strongly as physical contact. Another few steps and the seventeen long years of separation would have been forgotten.

But Ierii called and, as they hesitated, the moment was lost, the girl was with them, and her father close behind.

'Miron!' Ierii cried with delight. 'You are safe! Is Thyloss with you?'

He stared at her blankly. His joy at finding Quilla had driven all else from his mind. Dorran took his arm and slapped him on the back with pleasure.

'It is good to see you, my friend,' he said warmly. 'Thyloss thought you were in danger. He went looking for you.'

Miron looked at Quilla over the heads of the intruders. She smiled at him and he knew that Thyloss was not dead. He accepted it as though he had already known. But he could feel Quilla slipping away from him. The river of other people's needs flowed between them.

Quilla dropped her eyes and turned away, not trusting her expression. He was here at last! Surely they would be allowed some time together?

He answered the questions Ierii and her father asked as best he could. He had been in danger, but he was free now.

Quilla's eyes met his again and they both knew neither of them would ever be 'free.' But the word served well enough for the others.

The joy that Miron felt at finding Quilla and knowing that their son was alive was short-lived. Ma-ii was in danger and Thyloss was in Ma-ii.

'What kind of danger were you in?' Ierii asked anxiously, thinking of Thyloss.

Miron sat down and the others joined him. He realized that he was very tired. He sighed. Where should he begin?

'I think what has happened, though it is hard to tell, is that the Queen is crazed with grief over the death of her son and the priestesses of her cult are using this to seize absolute control of Ma-ii. It is not easy to explain. I felt great evil . . . a kind of monstrous distortion . . . they have taken certain elements of the old Bull Cult and given them greater significance than others so that the balance is destroyed; the cult no longer makes any kind of sense . . .'

'Surely the people will not allow this to happen?' Dorran said indignantly.

Miron shook his head.

'The people are behaving strangely, almost as though they are under the influence of some spell.'

Miron looked at Quilla.

'Something was at work in Ma-ii today that could not be explained in the way I am used to explaining things. If magic means that the mind and will of one can totally disrupt and dominate the mind and will of another, I am prepared to admit that I believe in magic, for this is what I experienced.'

Ierii was pale and agitated.

'Thyloss is down there!'

'A great many people are, my child,' Quilla said gently, putting her hand on the girl's shoulder. 'They need our help.'

'How can we help? Tell me!' cried Ierii desperately. 'I will do anything!'

'Shh . . .' Her father put his arm around her.

'We will find a way,' Quilla said confidently. 'We have not been brought together at this time for no reason.'

Miron buried his face in his arms. His knees were drawn up as he sat on the ground, his arms folded upon them.

'Miron is tired. He has been through much,' Quilla said gently. 'We must let him rest.'

'But meanwhile . . .' Ierii broke in impatiently.

'Meanwhile Thyloss can look after himself. He is not a helpless infant' – Quilla smiled – 'but a most capable young man.'

'But magic!' said Ierii anxiously.

'Magic is only effective against those who are unprepared, or do not want to resist it,' said Quilla.

Briefly Miron lifted his head and looked at her with weary eyes. Then he shut them and let his head fall. He was soon deep in a troubled sleep.

Thyloss knew the people of Ma-ii were in great danger, not only from the earthquake that Quilla had foreseen, but from the consequences of tampering with the ancient mysteries. He knew that he must work fast.

He spoke urgently with his family and all his closest friends, outlining the situation and suggesting a plan. Those who were trustworthy were given tasks to do, and soon, like seeds blown on the wind, his messengers were out among the people spreading the news of a meeting to be held on the Field of Challenge at sunset.

But other news was also in the air.

The young prince and the old king were to be buried at last in the funerary temple by the shore. The king was not to be given the dignity of the Death Challenge, but was to be buried without ceremony.

The townspeople were divided between their loyalty to the Queen and their curiosity to know why the young hero Thyloss summoned them to a meeting to be held at the same time as the funeral, and at the opposite side of the town. They were involved in choice and decision, and they were confused. Very few among them enjoyed decisions.

Thyloss could not find out where his father had gone, but as there were no reports of his having been found wounded or dead, he decided that he would trust the great lord to look after himself, and he would concentrate on what he felt to be his role. He became the centre of frenzied activity. People were constantly coming to him for advice.

He longed for a spell of time, however brief, when he could be alone to think. But many who had heard Ierii's warning of the coming cataclysm, and had witnessed the strange events on the Field of Challenge the day before, wanted to know if they should pack their belongings ready to leave the town, while others jeered at them and said that there was nothing to fear and that all would settle down again as soon as the proper ceremonies of burial had taken place. Had not the Black Thunderer, the greatest bull they had ever seen, been sacrificed? And since that moment the earth had not stirred in any way?

Miron's wife, although greatly troubled for her lord, tried to help Thyloss in every way she could. When she could see that he could handle no more questions, no more pushing, anxious crowds, she asserted herself and closed the doors of her house.

Thyloss sat down wearily; he heard the people hammering at the door; but he no longer cared that he could not answer them. The woman he had known as mother for as long as he could remember looked at him fondly, and then went to a cupboard that was very rarely used, and took something out, holding it carefully, as though it were very precious. She put it on the table before Thyloss.

'This used to be the Lady Quilla's,' she said. 'I know Miron would wish you to take it with you when you leave.'

'But you will come with me?' he said, looking up at her in alarm. 'We will all be going.'

'No,' she said. 'I will not leave without Miron. Take the children. I will stay.'

'But he may be already in the mountains!' Thyloss said.

'Then he will not need me,' she said softly, and turned away.

Thyloss was about to continue his protest, when his eye fell on the object she had placed before him, and he fell silent.

It was a bronze jar, plain and cylindrical, but on its lid was a bronze toad of exquisite workmanship, the warts made of rock crystals and pearl wedged skilfully into tiny shallow pits on the surface.

He gazed at it in amazement.

'Open it,' she said as she watched him from the other side of the room.

Wondering, he touched the lid and eased it off. Inside was a single circular baked-clay disc, each side engraved with signs, arranged in a spiral pattern. At the centre of one side was a flower.

'What is it?' he asked, turning it over and over in his hands.

He noticed that the signs were different on each side, though the spiral was the same size.

'It is a talisman. Use it to pray as you need it – but with care! It has power.'

'The signs are strange to me,' he said thoughtfully, looking closely.

'When you can read them, you will have power,' the woman said with confidence.

'Could Father read them?'

'No, I do not think so, though I saw him many times staring at it.'

'Did the Lady Quilla leave it as a gift, or did she leave it behind by mistake when she left in haste?'

'That I do not know. Before this time I have not touched it. I only know it was hers, and apart from you, it is the only thing of hers he has.' Thyloss rose and kissed her. They had spoken briefly of his new knowledge about Quilla and Mahra had shown no dismay. She had always been good to him, and now he realized how unselfish she was. There was no bitterness in her heart for the woman that she had always known her husband loved. She hugged him and returned his kiss and then turned away quickly, but not before he had caught the gleam of a tear in her eye.

'Do not leave it on the table,' she said, trying to maintain control of herself, but the tears so near the surface gave an edge of huskiness to her voice. 'Someone else might take it.'

He returned to the table, picked up the disc, and stood a long time with it in his hand, as he contemplated it.

Gradually the room seemed to fade away and the signs on the disc seemed to grow large and luminous. Imperceptibly his sense of reality changed, and he was drawn into the spiral, travelling down its pathways to the centre. Dimly he remembered the occasion when Quilla had shown Ierii and him that it was possible for Time not to exist. Between one heartbeat and the next, he slipped into that timeless state, and saw many things.

At the centre of the spiral he found the flower.

It seemed as though he was the centre of the flower, the

point of growth, and from him the petals of past, present, and future radiated.

He might have once thought of Time as a river, but now he knew that it was not. He knew that this moment and his present action were important in a way he could not have grasped with his ordinary consciousness.

This moment, any moment, is the growing point of the flower, and on it all things are centred.

That which threatened Ma-ii now had threatened other places at other times and would continue to do so until the world ended. Evil and loss were always there to be faced, and the only power he had was over how he faced it.

He shivered slightly as he carefully returned the disc to the jar.

He touched the beautiful toad as he fitted on the lid, and as he did so he received a charge of extraordinary energy, and knew that he could cope with all that lay before him.

Miron's wife could see the effect it was having on him, but not what he could see. She stepped forward and gave him his old leather pouch with the broad leather thong that went over his shoulder to carry it in, so that he could take it with him safely.

He could not yet bring himself to speak after the experience he had just had, but he looked at her gratefully, and did as she indicated.

13

As it was in the beginning . . .

When Miron was fully rested, he woke to find himself and Quilla at last alone together. She was sitting cross-legged, quietly watching him.

As he lay, suddenly fully awake, clean-eyed and alert, looking into her eyes, a flicker of a smile crossed her lips, a tinge of colour flushed her cheeks. She filled a cup of water and stooped over him, lifting his head with her left arm while she held the cup to his lips.

At first he accepted the cool liquid and then suddenly he pushed it aside, spilling it over her skirt as he rose on his elbow and seized her head to draw it down to his.

She lost balance and fell against him, hurting as he held her too harshly, too closely, his mouth on hers clumsy and fierce rather than tender.

'Miron,' her heart cried. 'Not like this! Not like this!' He released her and helped her to sit up again, drawing himself up at the same time. His eyes were dark.

'Why do you draw back?' he whispered. 'Why?'

'I do not draw back from you my love, but from that which possesses you.'

He put his head in his hands, a pulse beating loudly, in-sistently in his temples and in his throat. He had held Quilla as he had held the Queen, in desperation, not in love.

She stood up and paced about the cave, trying to still the agitation of her own heartbeats.

'There are shadows in you,' she said. 'I feel them. They are between you and me.'

'The years,' he tried to say, but she interrupted.

'No, not the years.'

He was silent, thinking of Nya-an.

Quilla stood still, looking at him. They had longed for each so much and now they were two strangers meeting for the first time. Had all that had been between them ever happened? What would it take for them to meet again as lovers? Perhaps, she thought, no more than a simple acknowledgement between them that they were no longer as they once had been.

'Come,' she said softly.

He followed her from the cave. As they walked they did not touch, although they longed to do so. Talking after so many years seemed inappropriate, so they only said what had to be said, as simply as possible.

She took him to her maze of white pebbles and when he saw it he told her how he had seen her walking it, when he was on the other side of the mountains bringing home the white bull.

She smiled at that.

'Do you believe me now when I talk of different realms of reality?'

'I accept many things I did not think possible a day or two ago, but what the explanation of them is . . . I am still not sure.'

She nodded and touched his hand.

'Wait here for me,' she said. 'I will walk the maze. I need its strength.'

She took her place at the entrance.

'Quilla . . . ' He started to speak and then hesitated.

'What is it Miron?' she said gently.

He stood silent, looking at her. The shadows of the trees were long. Evening was not far away.

She scarcely breathed, her eyes not leaving his, waiting for him to speak.

'I have not told you . . .'

He was thinking of the Queen but his thinking was now without shadow.

'You need tell me nothing', she said, smiling suddenly with relief, holding out her arms.

They forgot the Lady of the Lilies whose sacred grove enclosed them, and the dangers that even now seemed crouched to spring upon them.

The passion of their loving was the greater for all that had separated them and for all that had threatened them, but was the sweeter for the fact that they asked nothing of each other beyond the moment of their loving.

When they at last became aware of the world outside their love, the sun had already set, the last birds were winging home, and Dorran and Ierii had begun to worry about them.

The sun was low in the west when Ierii, who had gone alone to stand on a ledge where she could overlook the plain of Ma-ii, was startled to hear someone else upon the mountain.

Thinking at once of Thyloss, she rushed forward, but when the climbers came in sight she was disappointed to see they were only children, ragged and dirty and apparently very tired.

She called Dorran and together they went down the path to greet them. The girl hid behind the boy, trembling, but the boy faced them boldly, his hands clenched into fists, instantly on the defensive. Dorran smiled at once and showed his open hands.

'You need not fear us, boy,' he said kindly. 'We travel the same path.'

The boy looked relieved and flung himself upon the ground, exhausted; the girl thankfully sank down beside him.

Ierii thought she had seen the girl-child before, but could not think where. The boy was unknown to her.

'If you walk but a little farther,' she said, 'you will find food and water, and good straw beds to rest on.'

The children's eyes came to life at the thought of food and water. The day had been hot and they had been lost and wandering for the best part of it. But Dorran and Ierii could see that the effort required to climb the extra distance was too much for the girl.

'We will carry you,' Dorran said. 'Come, daughter, lead the way.'

The boy staggered to his feet and tried to lift the girl himself, but he was too weary and he had to leave the task to Dorran.

They were brought to Quilla's cave.

Neither Miron nor Quilla was in sight, so Dorran and Ierii took it upon themselves to play host and feed the children, giving them sweet water to drink from a gourd and goat's milk from an earthenware cup of great delicacy and beauty. Afterwards they laid them on the beds and covered them with loosely woven rugs.

Almost at once the boy was asleep, but the girl lay for a while staring with large sad eyes at the darkness in the corners of the cave. When she too was asleep, Dorran and Ierii left them.

'I wonder who they are and why they are so afraid,' Ierii said anxiously, wondering yet again what was going on down in the town.

'I know the girl,' Dorran said quietly.

'Who is she?'

'She is Princess Meri-an,' he said.

Ierii was startled. She knew now where she had seen her before, but the change from the cold, beautiful girl dressed in magnificent finery to the pathetic little waif on the mountainside was dramatic. Her expression was grave as she thought of the circumstances that could have brought about the change.

At sunset half the inhabitants of Ma-ii, dancing and singing, followed the Queen's procession to the funerary temple; while the rest followed Thyloss silently to the Field of Challenge.

Thyloss was surprised that the Queen, who must have known about the people he was gathering around him, should not try to stop him; surprised also that so many dared defy her and trust him.

While he was waiting for the last of the stragglers to crowd onto the field he fingered the bronze toad. He felt strengthened every time he touched it. He was glad he had it with him and said a silent prayer of thanks to Quilla for leaving it for him. For now it seemed as though all the long years had led to this moment, and all had been preparation just for this.

He experienced the tension and excitement that was so familiar to him when he had entered the Field of Challenge on other days, the crowd cheering, the Queen and her court at the horned shrine waiting to see his triumph or his death. Now it was he who took his place in front of her throne, he who surveyed the field and the gathering crowds.

Many had brought torches, and as the night shadows crept closer, more and more were fired until an eerie light shone around the heads of the anxious, restless people, while all else remained in darkness.

Old Ayan was beside Thyloss with some who had been taken into his confidence, and as time went on and still the people straggled onto the field, they urged Thyloss to start speaking. It was as though they could sense the shadow of danger creeping closer as every moment passed.

Thyloss stood on the throne and lifted his arms; Ayan, standing at his feet, held a torch so that his figure, lit from below, looked larger than life.

Within moments the crowd was silent, looking to him for comfort and advice. He looked over their heads at the holy mountain rising high above the plain. It shone in the full light of a rising moon.

He pointed, and as the crowd turned to follow the direction of his gaze, the moon in unimaginable silver splendour rose higher. The highest peaks glowed with an unearthly light.

The people took it as a sign, and, remembering the ancient moon rituals of their race, began to chant.

As the sound rose to greet the white moon, the harmony

of the many voices made the most beautiful music Thyloss had ever heard.

It rose and rose until it seemed as though it filled the sky and floated out towards the stars.

He imagined that anyone listening to the earth from another world beyond their knowledge would hear the sound and be moved by it to think the earth a beautiful, but a sad, place.

As the chanting died down, Thyloss began to speak, his voice ringing out loud and clear.

'There could not be many of you who have not been alarmed by the events of the past hours – the unnatural sacrifices – the actions of the Queen – the rumbling of the earth . . .'

There was a murmur of assent from the crowd.

'I have spoken with a great Seer and Prophet, and she has sent me to warn you . . .'

Someone cried out in fear.

'No. We should not fear. We should act. All that we have known is to be destroyed. The force that devastated our ancestors homes is building up again.'

A wail from many throats greeted this news.

But Thyloss continued steadily: 'A new life is assured us. There is a plateau in the mountains – there where the moon is shining. It will be a haven for us. There we will be safe.

'The Queen has overturned our traditions, mocked our sacred rituals, called on forces best left alone. Mighty retribution is due. We must leave before it falls.'

A shout of agreement went up from the crowd. Feet were stamped and fists raised.

Thyloss could feel the moment had come to turn them and lead them away. He felt powerful, exhilarated. But before he could give the order that would take them to safety – another sound was heard. A dreadful sound.

He had heard it before. It was the sound of thundering hooves. He remembered his vision.

But even as this knowledge struck fear to his heart, he saw Quilla and Miron hurrying to his side, pushing through the people.

Thankfully he turned to them.

'What is it?' he shouted. 'What is happening?'

They reached him just as the crowds gave way in panic before the charge of many bulls.

Behind the enraged animals came the priestesses . . . from their throats came the high ululation of the bull drovers' call . . . in their upraised hands whips snaked and cracked, stinging the backs of the terrified animals . . . driving them to frenzy, cutting off their retreat . . .

The funeral over, the Queen had turned her attention to her subjects on the Field of Challenge.

The air was filled with cries of pain and fear, the roar of angry, frightened bulls, the high weird screams of the deadly priestesses.

Everyone tried to escape; many, in panic, fell beneath the feet of their fellow men or the hooves of the beasts, and were trampled to death.

Miron, Quilla, and Thyloss alone kept their heads. Miron and Thyloss leapt onto the field, trying to turn the bulls, using all their skill.

Quilla stood on the throne where Thyloss had stood, lifted her arms, and shut her eyes. She tried to shut her mind to the confusion all about her, tried to lead her inner spirit from the shell of the woman Quilla to the level where she was free of body and strongly centred on that point of active Stillness, the growing kernel of Being, from which all power comes.

Twice she almost reached it, but the scream of someone in agony pulled her back. Should she leap onto the field as Thyloss and her love had, and turn the bulls as she had done so skilfully for so great a part of her life?

The question momentarily distracted her.

But the answer drove her back into herself.

Something else was needed.

Her isolation on the mountain had trained her for this moment. She was capable of an action that neither Thyloss nor Miron was capable of performing.

They must do what they were trained to do. She must do what she could do.

At the third attempt she knew that she had reached the level she needed for her work. She found the peace and calm and confidence that come from truly seeing the pattern of Being.

She beamed it with all the power she was now capable of to the people stumbling blindly on the field. She knew that their fear was feeding the fear of the bulls, and that they were helping to destroy themselves as the Queen had intended.

From Quilla rays of power came, and where they touched, the fear was less, the people worked with confidence to turn the bulls and to find their way out of the field.

But Quilla was not the only one who could beam thought energy. In opening a channel we may not be joined by one of the great, free Spirits of Light, but by one of the shadowy misshapen forms that have not progressed beyond their own lowest potential.

The fell priestesses knew this.

Before Quilla, in a place temporarily vacated by the frightened crowds, they took their stand, forming the pattern Thyloss had seen in his vision. They lifted their hands in unison and faced their palms to Quilla.

Fiercely they mustered their strength and willed the dark forces of hate and fear to be unleashed on the woman.

Pain seared Quilla's head and she felt her strength failing.

Desperately she clung to all that she had learned, desperately she tried to keep the channel of her Being open to the free Spirits of the high Spirit Realms . . . to love and trust and light . . .

The magic of the deadly women before her was strong.

She could feel the channel closing. Fear was closing in.

She fought it.

She staggered, but she rose again.

She could see the shapes of fear and dark rallying, drawn by the power of the priestesses.

She knew what she must do.

The beams she had been directing outwards she now turned inwards on herself. It was as though she drew the evil forces on the field with all her strength towards her own body, tempting them towards her, challenging them.

Miron looked round, in the midst of his struggle to hold the horns of a bull, in time to see Quilla transfigured with light, and the vibrating air above the field turn on itself and rush swirling inwards to the centre where she stood.

The bulls charged straight towards her, suddenly ignoring everyone else.

Miron was knocked aside, but he quickly recovered his balance and rushed towards her, his heart torn apart with the fear of losing her.

The priestesses lost formation and screamed, as the power they had invoked turned on them; it ignored their commands, and sent them scattering, hammering many of them into the ground.

Bewildered, but realizing that they were now safe, many people at the other end of the field turned to run towards the mountains. Others stayed, mouths wide with horror, as the dark tide reached the horned shrine.

Miron, with a speed that he had not used since he was a youth, reached Quilla and took her in his arms . . .

Together they went down as the beasts stampeded over them. Together they were buried under the debris of the horned shrine . . . the bulls, the last of the priestesses with them . . . the dark spirits departing as the force that had held them to earth lost its strength.

Thyloss stared, shocked beyond words.

He turned to run towards them, thinking that there would

still be time to pull them back to life . . . but as he turned he could see the sky over the northern ocean, and he stopped in his tracks. A ghastly and lurid red was spreading like a stain . . . like a sunset in a place where no sun had ever set before.

He stood stunned, not knowing what to make of it.

As he gazed, a giant black cloud rose from the centre of the horizon and began to lean across the sky towards him. His vision of the giant black bull returned. Voices louder than his heartbeats urged him from within to lead the people away to safety. His task was to rescue those he could, not mourn for those he could not.

Loudly his voice rang out above the now hushed and solemn crowd.

As one, they turned to follow him.

Behind them the sky grew redder and angrier, the black cloud higher and wider. Before them a broad pathway lined with strange glowing white stones showed them the quickest and easiest route to the holy mountain. They were the stones from Quilla's maze, which she and Miron had placed there on their way down the mountain. They glowed now with the light she had called upon at the moment of her triumph over the dark forces.

Ierii, Dorran, Princess Meri-an, and the boy Da-yi, stood on a ledge overlooking the sea plain and watched with horror the rise of the menacing cloud shaped like a huge black bull.

When Miron and Quilla had not returned at nightfall they had grown more and more anxious. Ierii had wanted to search for them, but Dorran insisted that she did not.

'They are together at last. They will come to no harm.'

They had tried to eat their evening meal calmly, tried to talk among themselves as though nothing was amiss, but it was not easy. After the meal the boy had wandered off, and it was he who called them to see what was happening in the town.

At first from where they stood it was not possible to make out exactly what was going on, but it was certain that there was a large gathering on the Field of Challenge. Hundreds of lights flickered, at first moving restlessly and then remaining stationary.

'I wonder what it is . . .' Ierii was saying curiously, when suddenly the pattern of lights changed violently. It was as though a sudden gust of wind had arisen near the eastern gate and at first the lights nearest the gate, and then progressively the others, were being blown about.

It was apparent to the watchers that what had been an orderly gathering was now a whirling mass of conflicting forces. Dorran held Ierii firmly back as she cried out that she was going down, that Thyloss was in danger.

'We are all in danger, child . . . our only way out of it is to do what we are most capable of doing. You cannot lead armies, fight bulls . . . but you can create an atmosphere of peace . . . you can guide people to see the other levels of reality on which they live . . . Quilla knew you had this quality. She knew you would be needed for it just as Thyloss is needed for his qualities. He will lead them out of danger. You will give them the strength to make the most of safety.'

Ierii was weeping.

'You speak as though Thyloss will be killed when his task is finished!'

'I did not say that. There will be many dangers to face when we leave here. He will be needed then too.'

'He will always be needed,' the little princess said quietly, slipping her hand into Ierii's.

'Come, Ierii, think only of his return, not of the danger that he is in. He needs strength from your thoughts – not weakness!'

'Mother of the Earth!' cried Da-yi. 'Look at the sky!'

They could see what Thyloss had not yet seen . . . the sky on fire above the far horizon.

'What is it?' Ierii gasped.

The princess trembled as she clutched the older girl's hand more tightly.

Dorran was silent. It is one thing to talk about conquering fear, and another to do it. He was deadly afraid. He had seen such a sight once before as a young boy on a ship off the coast of the island of Thera. His father had told him that it was caused by a volcanic eruption – the fiery depths of the earth bursting out into the air with tremendous violence. The position of the angry red and black of the sky now was exactly where Thera would be, just beyond the northern horizon.

'Mother of the Earth! The whole island of Thera must be going up!' And if this was the case it would not be long before they felt the shock of the earthquake that would inevitably accompany such an eruption. He remembered how with just a small eruption their ship had been tossed on an unbelievably turbulent ocean. With one so large that the glow of it could be seen so far away, the disturbance in the ocean would be cataclysmic. So this is what Quilla had foreseen. This is what they must flee from.

Unable to think what else to do, the four stood and watched with horror as the angry glow spread, and the dark cloud of ash and cinders rose higher and higher.

Below them on the plain most of the lights had been extinguished, but the few that were still bright seemed to be moving away from the field towards the mountain. In fact, a column of lights was crossing the plain towards them.

'Thyloss is coming!' Ierii cried with joy, but again Dorran restrained her from running down to meet him. His face was anxious as he looked at the sky.

Faint sounds were reaching them now, sounds of people crying and calling far below them ... and from across the sea ... a low crackling rumble that was like nothing they had ever heard before.

'Hurry!' whispered Ierii, willing Thyloss to move faster. 'Hurry! There is not much time!'

She knew that with an extraordinary clarity.

The princess was crying now, and the boy who had served her so devotedly all his life put his arms around her.

* * * *

Ierii's thoughts were in a turmoil. On one level she was anxious for Thyloss and afraid of the red and angry sky, the giant and mysterious earth that even now began to vibrate beneath them. But on another level her mind was working quickly and efficiently, thinking of the vision she had seen of a new home for the people of Ma-ii, planning the route they would take through the mountains.

She had never penetrated the mountains beyond the range on which they now stood, but she seemed to know them as intimately as she knew the little knoll that she used to use for meditation in her father's garden. Thoughts and images that had come to her during those quiet times now returned to her, and, for the first time, she understood them. It was as though they had been separate pieces of a puzzle given to her as she became ready for each piece, and now, when she was ready for the whole, she was given the key that made them all fall into place.

She forgot her fears, and stood straight, filled with confidence that she now knew what to do.

Thyloss would come and they would start a new life in a new place . . . as it was in the beginning . . .

What had started as an almost imperceptible vibration in the earth grew every moment into a powerful quake.

The people struggling up the mountainside felt the earth slip and shift beneath them, and would have scattered down to the plain again in fear had not Thyloss driven them on with his determination.

He knew that it usually made more sense to be on the open plain during an earthquake, but this time he had an overwhelming feeling that the plain was doomed and that their safety lay only in the mountains.

'Do not turn back!' he shouted urgently. 'Believe me! Trust me! We must go on!'

Some were too afraid and could not trust him. They turned back, but those that followed him did so for the strength and the conviction in his voice. He apparently knew something they did not know, in a way they did not understand, and they trusted him.

The princess screamed as she saw the sea rise up from its bed and, red as blood, form into a wave as wide as the horizon.

Horrified, they watched it as it rose and rose and then, break and roll towards the shore.

The cloud was over the moon now and the only light came from the red glow in the north and its reflection on the gigantic wave.

Those who were still on the plain could not see it coming, but those who had already reached the slopes of the mountain could. Ierii and her little group could hear their cries, and they shuddered at the sound.

The bedrock beneath the plain was cracking, boulders were falling off the mountain. And then the wave hit the shore and roared like thunder as it poured over the town, smashing everything in its path, covering everything with a flood of turbulent and violent water.

The people still on the plain were caught; screaming, they were swept away by the earth's impersonal need for renewal.

'Do not look back!' Thyloss shouted, his voice with unusual strength carrying above the sound. 'We must keep going up!'

Now the people who had stayed with him could see why the mountains were safer than the plain; and they struggled on with every reserve of energy they could muster.

The group that finally reached Quilla's cave was much, much smaller than the group that had met on the Field of Challenge.

They were exhausted and dirty, but they were alive.

The earth shook no more.

Ierii met them some way down the path and flung herself upon Thyloss. Almost too weak to withstand the weight of her body, he staggered and then held on to her as a drowning man might hold to a post or a log he found within reach.

'Thyloss,' she sobbed. 'Thyloss!' She kissed him frantically again and again, sobbing his name, thinking of nothing but that he was alive. At first he did no more than hold to her, and then his lips reached for hers and in a long and desperate kiss he showed her that his need for her was as great as hers for him.

It was Dorran who brought them back to what was happening on the mountain. He pulled at Ierii's arm. At first she took no notice because she was aware of nothing but Thyloss, and then she tried to ignore the insistence of his interruption because she did not want to be aware of anything but Thyloss, but eventually Dorran's voice could not be ignored. She looked up and saw why her father was so agitated.

Their ordeal was not yet over. The dark bull-shaped cloud from the distant volcano, which had grown with every moment more and more monstrous, still reached for them. The wind was carrying its baneful influence towards them. Fine sulphurous ash was falling and the fumes from it were threatening to suffocate them. Finding themselves choking, those who had sunk down upon the mountainside to rest, staggered to their feet. Those who could not were dragged up by others. Stumbling and coughing, their lungs burning and aching, they struggled under the guidance of Dorran to Quilla's once secret and solitary cave.

Once most of the people were inside, Thyloss and Ierii worked to draw skins across the mouth to shut out as much of the drifting ash and the sulphurous smell as possible, and then they helped the last stragglers into the cave before they themselves sought shelter.

Inside they realized that the danger of suffocating was almost as great as it was outside. The cave was too small to hold so many people and the discomfort of so many bodies pressed together did nothing to allay the fear that was once again threatening to overwhelm the crowd. Thyloss was reminded of the restless agitation of wild animals captured and penned together, building up for a sudden violent bid for freedom. Those nearest the entrance were already pushing to get out into the air, forgetting that the air was now unbreathable.

Suddenly Ierii remembered something, or thought she did, though later she realized it was no memory but a prompting from the Invisible Realms. She 'remembered' that behind a curtain in the corner of the cave was a crack in the rock and a natural tunnel that led to a vast cavern system. Pressed close against Thyloss she told him of it.

Weary as he was he took control again and in a voice that rose commandingly above the sobbing and the complaining, demanded that a passage be made for him. He held the torch Dorran had lit above his head and squeezed through the crowd. He pulled the curtain aside and saw that Ierii was right.

He turned back to the crowd and told them in a strong, calm voice that in a few moments they would have room to breathe if they allowed themselves once more to be led by him.

The mood of the crowd changed at once. All eyes were on the handsome figure at the entrance to the tunnel, the flame-light flickering on his face.

'Thyloss,' they whispered with dry and aching throats. 'Thyloss!' Once again the young bull leaper was their hero and they trusted him to lead them to safety.

They waited in silence and hope as he checked out the tunnel and cheered when he returned lifting his fist above his head to show that he bore good news. Then he issued orders sharply, firmly and one by one he managed to get them to squeeze through the narrow opening and stumble down the dark passage beyond.

As they reached the great open space of the cavern the ones still in Quilla's small cave could hear them shouting with relief.

The night passed and Thyloss and most of the people found that they were so exhausted they could sleep in the strange cavern, the flickering of many torch lights playing on the weird and twisted shapes of the rocks around them. But Ierii lay close against Thyloss, her head on his shoulder, his arm around her, unable to sleep. The burden of what Quilla expected of her was heavy, but she found she was thinking of the future with a courage that surprised her: she found that she no longer feared responsibility, for Quilla's teaching now made sense to her. In the midst of chaos and suffering they had not been alone: they had had guidance.

In the morning, before Thyloss was awake, Ierii ventured out. What she saw chilled her heart.

Below on the stricken plain lay the once proud, busy town of Ma-ii, silent and unmoving. Broken walls pushed up from black and slimy ash. The sea had retreated behind its ancient shoreline again but the azure blue to which she was accustomed had given way to a heavy leaden grey. The beach, once of white and gold, was filthy with grey pumice and sodden with wet soot.

Tears filled her eyes.

Beyond the town every green and living thing upon the once fertile plain had disappeared. A pall of black ash was over everything.

It lay even on the ground beside her as she stood, its acrid smell fouling the sweet mountain air.

On the plain and against the base of the mountain range it was thickest. Vineyards and orchards were no more than dark sticks reaching blindly to the air, and where there had been fields of living grain, of wheat and barley, there were now flat featureless plains of black dust.

She felt a touch on her arm and turned to find Thyloss behind her. He held her as she wept, looking over her head at the scene she had witnessed.

'Mother of the Earth!' whispered Dorran coming out of the cave, his heart breaking, knowing that no living thing could have survived that deadly falling cloud. The plain was a desert.

They were joined, one by one, by others. Stiff and dazed the people crawled from the depths of the cave and stared at the devastation.

At first they were silent, gazing around at the scene, looking for some familiar landmark to give them comfort and a sense of the continuation of all that they had known. When they found none, most began to weep. Those who had family or friends clung to them, keening together. Of those who were alone, some began to scream and call and run about, not yet realizing the finality of their loss, wanting to believe that there was still a chance that those they loved would be amongst the people on the mountain and not on the silent plain.

Some drew aside from the crowds, wanting to be alone, keeping their suffering to themselves.

Where they stood the fatal ash was thin compared to that upon the plain, but farther up the range it was thinner yet.

'Look!' cried Ierii suddenly, pointing.

On the slope beyond the Crystal peak, the slope facing inwards to the plateau, which had been sheltered from the wind that had blown the night before, the tough mountain plants were still alive.

A small white lily shone from a cleft. She took Thyloss by the hand and pulled him towards it.

'Come,' she called to Meri-an and Da-yi, to Dorran and the others.

At first only a few came, but soon others followed until there was a whole group gathered around the mountain lily.

'See,' she cried, 'it is a sign!'

Meri-an began to laugh.

'A sign!' she echoed Ierii.

'A sign!' others began to murmur.

Meri-an clapped her hands and began slowly to dance, to turn, to spiral around the fragile lily.

One by one the stricken people joined her until the ledge on the mountain was full of people crowding together, weeping and laughing and singing, turning and turning in the confined space around the lily.

Thyloss drew Ierii aside from the dance, pulled her gently after him until they were hidden from the others behind a rock. His arms rested on either side of her, trapping her with her back to the stone, looking into her eyes with an expression that made her flush and lower hers.

At last he kissed her, his arms leaving the rock face and tightening around her.

The long years that had been between them were in the kiss, and the long years that were to come.

Notes

1. During what is sometimes called the Protopalatial Period on Crete *c.*2000-1700BC, the Minoan Civilisation was at its height. In approximately 1700BC an earthquake destroyed all the magnificent palaces on the island, but most of them were rebuilt and Minoan life continued strong and vigorous. There was another period of widespread destruction *c.*1450BC, possibly coinciding with a gigantic volcanic eruption on the island of Thera (Santorini) 90 kilometres north of Knossos. After this, most of the Minoan sites were abandoned and the Achaeans conquered and dominated a weakened land. However, isolated pockets of Minoan civilisation continued for some time in the mountains and the plateaux of the interior. In the limestone mountains surrounding the plateaux there are many and extensive caves used for sanctuary and religious purposes. I explored such a cave in 1987 which had artefacts from Neolithic, through Minoan, Doric and Byzantine times to the present day.

2. The labyrinth or maze has long been associated with the Minoans in Crete. The legend of the Minotaur, a monster half bull, half man, produced by the unnatural coupling of Queen Pasiphaë with a bull, is well known. It was imprisoned in a labyrinth and fed sacrificial youths and maidens until Theseus killed it and found his way out of the place using a thread given to him by the princess Ariadne. This maze had to be one of the second type mentioned in chapter 6 – meant to confuse and terrify. Both types have been found depicted on seal rings, coins and other artefacts from Egypt, Crete and most ancient cultures. The first type, Quilla's type, with no dead ends, but a single, winding, twisting path to the centre, has been extensively used in ecclesiastical architecture. Many a Medieval

Christian Cathedral or Abbey has a pavement maze of this type for pilgrims to walk while they adjust from the material world to the spiritual, e.g. Chartres and Bayeux in France; S. Maria-di-Trastavera in Rome, S. Vitale in Ravenna, Italy; Ely Abbey in Cambridgeshire, England. While I was writing "The Lily and the Bull" I laid out a rage, like Quilla's, with sea-rounded pebbles in my garden. I walked it at dawn every day to get the inspiration for the book. The hedge maze at Hampton Court, London, is of the kind meant to tease and confuse.

3. Quilla as young bull-acrobat and "Lord of the Sun" appears in my trilogy "Guardians of the Tall Stones".

About Moyra Caldecott

Moyra Caldecott was born in Pretoria, South Africa in 1927, and moved to London in 1951. She married Oliver Caldecott and raised three children. She has degrees in English and Philosophy and an M.A. in English Literature.

Moyra Caldecott has earned a reputation as a novelist who writes as vividly about the adventures and experiences to be encountered in the inner realms of the human consciousness as she does about those in the outer physical world. To Moyra, reality is multidimensional.

For more information about Moyra and her books, please visit www.moyracaldecott.co.uk